HISTORIES OF MGO

EDWIN CALLIHAN

"The Womb" was originally published in *Scare Street Night Terrors Vol. 14 2021*

"He Who Knocks 'Em Dead" was originally published in *Weirdpunk Books Sub Club Zine 2023*

"Need a Light" was originally published in *Midnight Tales #7 Fall 2022*

"Necrozoic" was originally published in *Midnight Tales #4 Spring 2021* + adapted as an audio drama on *The Lurking Transmission Podcast*

"Born Under the Master's Spell" was originally published in *In the Shadow of the Horns: A Black Metal Horror Anthology Vol; 1*

"Higher Forms of Voyeurism" was originally published in *Grow Worms Issue 1*

"Summoning the Pale Aristocracy" was originally published in *Into The Crypts of Rays: A Black Metal Horror Anthology Vol. 2*

Castaigne
publishing

Copyright © Castaigne Publishing 2024

ISBN: 979-8-9891571-3-6

Printed in The United States of America

First Edition

Cover Art by Andrew Wesley Bennett

PRAISE FOR EDWIN CALLIHAN

"Callihan tells stories like a grindcore band creating the soundtrack for Tales from the Crypt. Visceral, occult, and unique; Histories of Mgo is an elder god that refuses to turn down its stereo."

— —DAMIEN CASEY *AUTHOR OF CHURCH OF SKATAN, 28 DAYS SASSIER*

"Edwin Callihan's Histories of Mgo is the dread-riddled, anxiety-inducing collection of inward-facing horror you need on the top of your to-be-read pile."

— —SCOTT BRYAN WILSON *AUTHOR OF TRVE KVLT, KILL MORE*

"Callihan writes with the vision of a rust belt Ligotti, equally concerned with the slow rot of poverty and the liminality of the dark."

— — COY HALL *AUTHOR OF GRIMOIRE OF THE FOUR IMPOSTORS, THE HANGMAN FEEDS THE JACKLE, THE PROMISE OF PLAUGE WOLVES*

"These stories don't go where you think you want them to until it happens, and you realize you weren't meant to second guess. Edwin's prose style conjures the kind of raw imagery that imprints upon the reader leaving a lasting mark long after the story is through. This fresh voice is one we'll be hearing from for a long while indefinitely."

— -JOHN WAYNE COMUNALE AUTHOR OF
DEADLINE AND *THE CYCLE*

CONTENTS

FOREWORD
EVAN DEAN SHELTON

Time is the greatest devil of them all. Time is the outer god, the Old One that devours every one of us. A great horrific sculptor that crafts monstrosities, whittling away at the shapes of us until we are malformed. And then devoured. But in all things there is an ecology. What time eats it also shits into the great flow of existence. Bathing in it. Drinking it. Standing in the precipitation of it. An eldritch ecology. You understand how these things work, I'm sure. Ecology, Dear Receiver, is cyclical. As is everything.

"...works every time..."

Within the pages of Histories of Mgo, you will find that time is an amorphous lurching omnipresence. A great blind undulating wailing horror that looms over all, tossing us about on seas of uncertainty, crashingdown upon us in destructive and harrowing waves that leave nothing but drowned and rotten memory. Mgo as a place is an island in this sea. A spot of firmament in a hungry and chaotic abyss. Cling to this-

precipice as tight as you want, but I assure you the waves are coming back, and next time they'll be bigger, and swimming with worse horrors...

"The wrong world's out there."

Despite what the khakis may have you believe, Dear Receiver, horror fiction is an art form with an agenda: to horrify you. Edwin Callihan is a writer that understands that agenda well, and crafts his stories accordingly. For me personally, some of the scariest stories I have ever read are in this collection, and I've been around the block a bit. But not this block. Don't go walkin around here. For fuck's sake, you realize we're in Mgo?? My point here is that for me one of the most affecting and scary things about a story is environment. Sure a good and terrible antagonist is great and can be just as affecting for some, butfor me when an environment can't be trusted, when the landscape itself is an unknowable horror...that gets me. Edwin is a master of atmosphere, of making the very ground underneath and air that surrounds an adversary. He writes landscapes I do not want to explore. That makes every step taken by his characters another hair raised on the back of my neck. That's horror. If you want horror you're in the right place. The most wrong place you could ever be. Mgo.

"THE GEOLOGIC TIME SCALE ABUSED BY HUMANKIND AND THEIR DENIAL CANNOT CONTINUE."

Somebody's always talkin about "who's the next Lovecraft", and that's a silly way to frame this conversation. There is no

Next Lovecraft, no one writer who has come along and solely inherited thetorch. Nor will there ever be. That's not how this works. But let's jabber on anyway. So a lot of folk cite Thomas Ligotti, and that's fair. Ligotti certainly brought new shades of awful to cosmic horror and brought things up to date for his time at the keyboard, stripped away a bit of the stodgy academia andreplaced it with a hollow and howling yuppie upper middle class evil. But Ligotti's work is decades oldnow, Dear Receiver, and exists in that brief period after the sixties and before this modern era of neverending surveillance and social media squawking. It also exists in a world of professionals and huge houses, where it has any real human element at all. Edwin Callihan's work encompasses as much of the great expanse as one can fathom, from the psychedelic microscopic sickness swimming in the rotting viscera and rank latrines left in the wake of our wars to the planet sized horrors that hunger in the blackness beyond space where only eyes rolled back into their own skulls can see. It's all here, baby. And being terrifyingly dissolved within this hungry maelstrom are real people, humans, characters whosedesperate, grease-stained and intoxicated lives look at lot closer to my own than anything I've ever read inLovecraft or Ligotti. Edwin Callihan grounds cosmic horror in a way that's hypnotic and familiar. Familial. Like when your cousin talks you into doin' weird drugs.

"The worst of all possible worlds. I'll see you in Hell."

Histories of Mgo is like a map of a fractal seen in a nightmare and barely remembered. A suggestion of meaning, a hint of connective tissue, a tiny glimpse of a mind-shattering existential conspiracy bestunknown. A circular, cyclical, psychedelic experience. The span of these stories will take you across the bladed edge of time, bleeding out over the abyssal expanse of primordial ooze underneath the universe. Mgo is a pustule in time. A volcanic edifice of spuming horror, surrounded by the great ravenous sea of nothing, forever. A refuge, for some. Welcome.

For Taj, Soren, and Brittany.

"A thousand times I had this dream,
    The flag was high, I heard a scream
    That cut through the still of the night
    Just like a knife
    But that was yesterday,
    The darkness has gone away
    I stand on the edge, and I pledge my life"
—The Last Command, W.A.S.P.

THE WOMB

I looked up at the neon sign: Jef's Rare Books. The sign hung vertically above the entrance and radiated a candescent purple that flickered against the colorless concrete walls. A bell rang when I walked through the doorway, and an elderly gentleman popped up like a jack-in-the-box behind the counter.

"Howdy, looking for anything in particular or just looking?"

"Just looking, Jef," I said.

"Emil?" Jef adjusted his glasses, bringing my anonymity into focus. "I didn't even recognize you with the beard. I haven't seen you in ages."

"Don't have much free time these days, especially with the wife."

"Wife? Well, congratulations. Any kids yet?"

"God, no. I'm married, not insane."

"Can't say I blame you. The wrong world's out there."

"Yeah, and I prefer to spend my free time here rather than changing shitty diapers."

"Well then, I won't keep you."

The mildew of the yellow paper wafted when I flipped through the bins. Dust shimmered in the beams of light cast from the tiny windows. Pulp magazines and golden age comics books filled the containers as if I had stumbled upon a lost treasure.

Loose stacks of old newsprint and pamphlets scattered across a table, some dating back as far as the late nineteenth century. Mostly just manifestos of obscure political factions before the two-party system snuffed out any questionable ideology. One pamphlet caught my attention. Typed across the top in Old English calligraphy was the title, The Womb. Directly under the title: a large black circle smacked on the middle of the cover. Simple enough layout, but my gaze fell victim to the circle's swirling blackness as if I were staring into a planet-devouring black hole.

Time crawled in this dark vortex until I heard books fall from the shelves down the hall. Drool trickled down my chin while I was under the strange hypnotic stupor. I don't know why I carried it to the counter. I lacked the will to leave it behind. None of that matters now, does it?

"Find anything?" Jef prepared to ring up my purchase, but when his eyes met that black circle, he paused. His pupils dilated, and his teeth chattered, staring into the blackness.

"Jef?" I said his name a few more times before shouting it. "Jef, you okay, man?"

"W-what?" Jef adjusted his glasses. "Where did you find this?"

"It was in a stack back beside the bins." I pointed back down the hallway.

"It's not for sale."

LORETTA WASN'T enthusiastic about my plans for the night. She never was much of a night owl or a beer drinker. Lately, she was never much for anything except procreating.

"But I'm off tomorrow," she said. "I thought we could try again."

"Let me take a rain check." I rolled my eyes. "I was going to drink a beer and check out this shit from Jef's."

"A beer? You mean twelve?" She scoffed, and her voice grew louder. "And then you're going to stagger into bed with your dick hard, hoping to get at least three minutes of fucking?"

"Would it kill you to sleep alone? I know I'd kill to be alone for once."

Silence bled into the ambiance of our locked stares until her eyes brimmed with tears. She turned around with a loud sigh, disappearing into the darkness of the hallway.

There is no happily ever after. We eat, sleep, and fuck according to the necessity of survival. We can flower our primal instincts with fancy words like love and hate, but deep down, we know it is all part of the program. I was in denial too until I read *The Womb*.

I downed a beer. It would have been easier to shotgun, but I was trying to be responsible. I cracked open another one, sat down in my recliner, and grabbed the brown paper bag from Jef's. There it was, practically fell into my lap. *The Womb*. I heard the name in a multitude of chattering whispers.

No, the voice was my own, wasn't it? At the time, I thought nothing of it. A timeworn image of a nameless woman shrouded in a dark cloak stared back from the opening page.Long locks fell from the deep hood obscuring a shadowy face. An inscription ran across the borders along with droplets and flecks of red ink.

The Mother, the master.
She bears no weakness.

The last warm swig of my beer went down with a hefty gulp. I ran my finger across the passage and the specks of red ink smeared across the page. Upon reading, I heard music, a climactic melody in my head and the finale in a vacuous symphony conducted by emptiness. My thoughts were fulgurated and burst into fragments. Each one plucked from a cold abyss by some external sentience.

My beer clanked against the empty bottles. I looked up, and Loretta was standing in black panties and a white T-shirt that thinly veiled her breasts.

"Come to bed, Emil. I'm cold."

A muggy summer and the beads of sweat reflected in the lamplight suggested a different temperature, but I wasn't going to argue. We did enough of that. I chugged my last beer and followed her into the dark.

HOT BREATH EXHALED against my chest while she rested her head there. I worried about what the neighbors heard that night. Love and hate became tethered in their primal nature.

My eyelids refused to fall while my adrenaline lingered. Bodiless voices recited the passage in endless repetition. *The Mother, the master. She bears no weakness.* The orchestral sounds of nothingness rose in a triumphant roar and disquieted images materialized. The black circle obstructed my vision and spiraled into a translucent haze. Pels of blinding light peeked from behind the mass, and I wondered what waited behind the closed portal.

Something moved between Loretta's legs. Serpentine movements slithered under the sweat-drenched bed sheets onto my calf, and I could feel a slime trail like a salted slug. It oozed up my thigh toward my stomach. The bloody appendage reared its eyeless head like a mutant cobra. A single orifice opened with jagged fangs, dripping thick black fluid. Once it struck my belly button and started sucking, the colors of reality evaporated, and my body followed. My skin cracked, and my organs collapsed into mush as my blood ran dry.

Dreaming or drunk?

None of that matters now, does it?

SIZZLING bacon and the smell of freshly brewed coffee permeated the house. Loretta wore my button-up shirt, unbuttoned, in her underwear, and her right ass cheek hung out the side. As I walked in, she plucked the wedgie out and smiled back. She fixed a plate of food and slid it on the kitchen table. The opening titles to an episode of The Three Stooges blared from the small television mounted above the table.

"Hey, love, you sleep all right?"

"Ugh, yeah." I rubbed my heavy eyes. "What's the occasion?"

"What do you mean?" She smiled.

"Nothing, I guess."

Surfing the television channels, I found a what's-her-name news anchor rambling on about a murder downtown; nothing new for a town next to hell.

"Witnesses have stated that it is a bloody mess inside Jef's Rare Books, and rumors are already circulating that there are connections to organized crime and possibly, a local cult. Sixty-nine-year-old bookstore owner, Jef Landry, has been in business for forty years without ever being subject to violence and is known for his generosity in the community but was he involved in something more sinister? Authorities have yet to comment, but we will continue with updates."

"Isn't that—" Loretta's words escaped her lips.

I didn't respond.

The knock at the door broke the stillness.

The woman at the door seemed too attractive to be a cop with her curvy figure and unblemished skin but the neutral-colored suit, tightly pulled back hair, and impenetrable lensed shades suggested otherwise.

"Mr. Masterson?" She flashed her badge. "Detective Silvia."

"Yes? Something I can help you with?"

"You're familiar with Jef Landry, correct?" she said as I nodded. "You were at his store yesterday, correct?"

"Yeah, I can't believe what happened."

"Tragic, I know. I'm trying to piece together a timeline of the events leading up to Jef's murder. What time did you last encounter Mr. Landry?"

"Late afternoon, early evening. Any idea who would do this to him?"

"No." Her shades slid down the bridge of her nose. "Do you?"

"Of course not."

"Did he ever mention anybody following him?"

"No, but it's been a few years since I've been out there."

"Right. Why's that?"

"Working a lot, married—you know how that goes?"

"No, I don't, *actually*. Any kids?"

"Kids?"

"Yes, do you have children, Mr. Masterson?"

"Nope. No kids."

"Must be nice, huh?"

"Wouldn't you know it?" I laughed.

"Yes, I would." She grinned back.

DETECTIVE SILVIA LEFT a card and told me to call if I had more information I could remember. I didn't mention *The Womb. Why would I?*

Loretta didn't speak for the rest of the day. She must have sensed I was a bit off. I felt like vomiting up dog shit. I thought about Jef, and my curiosity ate away at the back of my brain like festering maggots. I left the house without saying a word.

DOWNTOWN WAS the same gray landscape. I strolled the sidewalks through globules of people, and I started counting the whooshing of cars across the rain-soaked streets. A woman in a long black overcoat with a deep hood exited the crowd. Her black locks flowed in the breeze exposing a drooping pale face with each gust. *Was it some cheap Halloween mask?* I thought.

Empty black pools sunk far into her skull, and she stared at me from the other side of the crosswalk. Pedestrians faltered upon her, and a large delivery truck burst across the view. She vanished.

Jef's store, now lined with yellow caution tape and a couple of patrol cars by the entrance, had fallen victim to the rest of the town's failure. An officer stood against the cruiser's hood sipping on a coffee, and I approached with a friendly wave. Already irritated, he lowered his coffee and sighed. "Listen, buddy. I'm not answering any questions. Like I told the last reporter, *get fucked*. You can quote me on that one, all right?"

"I'm not a reporter. I'm friends with the owner."

"You mean, *was*." He sipped his coffee and noticed I wasn't disappearing. "Look, you need to talk to the team on the case. This is just my beat."

"Right. What happened exactly?"

"You didn't hear this from me," he said softly but eager. "Let's just say they had a hard time getting an ID on the guy. If it wasn't for his fucking name on the building, I doubt they would."

"What do you mean?"

"He was splattered all over the fucking place." The officer's eyes oscillated, securing his perimeter, and he sunk his face closer to mine. "Apparently, your friend was involved in some freaky-deaky cult shit too."

"Like what?"

"I don't know exactly, but looks like he was fucking around with the wrong one. At least, that's what I heard down at the precinct."

"Jef? There's no way."

"Hey." He raised his hands in an innocent gesture. "You didn't hear any of this from me."

Splattered all over the fucking place seemed to cover most of what I needed to know.

The jagged skyline drowned in the twilight while the sun sank behind the city's silhouette. I had not received one missed call from Loretta. I expected at least a text but nothing. The parking garage's fluorescent lights flickered and hummed. My footprints echoed, and distant cars were revving their engines on the upper levels. My car was parked by its lonesome space facing the interior of the garage. A figure fiddled with the driver's side windshield, and I shouted at them to back the fuck up.

Her face was a penumbra as it reared up from underneath the hood. If it wasn't a mask, her skin was hanging off her skull. She attempted to smile, but the loose skin could barely lift the cheeks. She darted around the corner, and her crooked posture vanished into the labyrinth of automobiles. A flyer was secured under the windshield wiper and covered in red speckles, which I now know was blood.

She bears no weakness, Emil.

Speeding down the highway, I weaved between the other cars. They applauded my driving with honks and flying middle fingers from their windows. I strangled the steering wheel with a viselike grip until my thumbs formed blisters. Sirens approached, accompanied by flashing red and blue lights glowing in my mirrors. *Fuck.*

I pulled over to the shoulder of the highway. The passing cars were bright blurs in the newborn night. A set of legs stepped out of the police car while the blue and red luminosity danced in all the surrounding reflective surfaces. My window rolled down, and a subtle cleavage revealed from a gray and black suit greeted me. A familiar face craned down, and oddly enough, she was smiling.

"Detective Silvia, how are you?"

"Imagine this, Mr. Masterson. Are you a fan of NASCAR?"

I couldn't tell if this was casual joking or the sarcasm was prowess, so I laughed it off. "No, Detective. I just haven't talked to my wife all day."

"Oh, of course. You miss your wife. I understand that, but—"

"Well, it's not that," I interrupted. "I'm just concerned. She hasn't tried to call or text, and I think somebody is following me."

"Followed by who?"

"I'm not sure. A woman. A weird-looking woman."

"Well, you ain't bad lookin', but what were you doing downtown?"

"Shopping." *Was Detective Silvia following me, too?* I thought.

"If you're trying to snoop around my investigation, then we are going to have more problems than being followed."

"I was curious about Jef, that's all. I wasn't playing detective. Just curious."

"Curiosity killed the cat," she said, grinning. "Your friend Jef was torn to shreds. Obliterated, and it's not every day a pack of wild animals break into a used bookstore, am I right?"

"Right."

"Now, get the hell out of here and stay away from my crime scene." She stepped from my window.

"Oh, and Emil."

"Yeah?"

"Take care." She winked, strolled back to her vehicle, and sped around me before I could even start my ignition. I struggled to focus, so I waited a few moments at the shoulder, watching traffic interpolate from exit ramps. The automobiles followed signs and stoplights and merged into a collective of vehicular order without thinking. I called Loretta and stepped on the gas.

No answer.

THE DRIVE TOOK LONGER than anticipated, turning down back roads and neighboring cul-de-sacs to shake off whatever was following me or at least ease the anxiety. It didn't work. I could sense a *disruption*.

Our house looked abandoned and attracted the shadows of the dimly lit street. The front door was slightly ajar, so I creaked in and flipped on the light switch. The television was still on the news station in the kitchen, but the sound was on mute. Loretta's keys and phone laid on the kitchen table alongside *The Womb*. Loretta couldn't withstand the dominion of the black circle's invitation. *Did it get her too?* I thought.

Her car was still in the garage. I had hoped to find her in there, thinking maybe she had passed out—or worse. I couldn't decide if I was relieved or concerned at discovering an empty car.

The door leading from the garage to the kitchen smacked shut. I jumped up and peeked over the top of the car. Shadows moved at the slit of light bleeding from the bottom of the door. I heard the muffled sounds from inside the kitchen that sounded like the screeching cries of an infant. I darted to the door and shoved through it only to find the same empty kitchen. The television volume was to the maximum.

Authorities are currently tracking down the prime suspect responsible for the murder of Jef Landry yesterday evening. Police are urging citizens to provide any information they have on the suspect.

The police sketch was close enough, possibly a little too flattering considering my age.

The channels played roulette until the screen hissed with white noise fading into surveillance footage.

At the counter, Jef snatched *The Womb* from my hands. I smiled and waved at the camera as if I knew I was watching at that moment. I yanked Jef across the counter and plowed my fists into his face. There was no audio, but I heard his screams as I pulverized his body with my feet. I crouched on him and clawed into his flesh with my hands. Blood puddled around Jef while his arms and legs kicked, struggling to break free like some helpless prey. The final moments of the footage show him—what was left of him—pulled offscreen, sliding across the floor in a trail of gore. I reached over the counter and grabbed *The Womb* before the footage faded back into white noise.

Quiet and calm, I walked into the living room. I sat down and attempted to read this cursed pamphlet, but all of the pages were blank. There was nothing to be read, nothing to be understood. I called the police, but not to confess, I assumed they would be finding my whereabouts soon enough.

I asked to speak to Detective Silvia. "Detective who?" the voice on the other end asked before cutting off into a solid dial tone.

My breath fell into shallow gasps while my heart thumped against my rib cage. A clatter crashed through the house, and

I could hear somebody slug against the walls coming closer down the hallway.

A shadow emerged, and the harsh lamplight made her look like she was sitting around a campfire. We had never been so close. The depth of her wrinkles were deep ridges that ran across her face into her drooping cheeks.

Things squirmed and writhed under her loose facial skin, and I heard them whisper, "The Mother, the master."

"She bears no weakness," I said.

Bashing her with the lamp or even strangling her crossed my mind, but I couldn't run anymore. This was always the plan.

I rose and examined her face. The fleshy face-shroud oozed between my fingers, and I pulled them apart like dough. The skin ripped between the eyes, lips, and chin in one giant tear. Before I blinked, I stared at the face of an abyss and the gaping maw overflowing with thrashing tendrils of pure darkness. Each one of them was reaching to extract light. Her cloak dropped to the ground, and she vanished like a magician's assistant. The familiar hollow melody from the first time I opened *The Womb* erupted like the entire orchestra was in my living room, but I was finally alone.

My body slumped, and my knees gave out. I dropped to the floor, hitting hard against the cold linoleum. My limbs contorted into a fetal position, and each finger and toe crooked inward. The hairs on my body singed away from my crawling flesh while the rest of my physical body broke down at a cellular level. Residual black liquid puddled where I once stood, bubbling with my last gasps of consciousness.

Thoughts eroded, and self-awareness drifted away like the decay of dead stars. I forgot myself in some distant unborn nebula and only felt eternity's reflection of pain until it faded as well. Darkness swirled to the sounds of nothingness that had reached the crescendo. *The Womb was the Mother*, and she absolved her mistake. *She bears no weakness.*

From the moment my gaze fell into the chasm of darkness on that pamphlet, *The Womb* knew and hosted several corporeal forms—Detective Silvia, the strange-faced lady, the pamphlet itself, and hell, even Loretta—to manipulate reality's ebb and flow. Jef knew his time was due, but he resisted, so *The Womb* used me just as it had used him and the other ignorant disciples among the afterbirth. All of us are children of incestual copulation between time and space. The Womb illuminates our only path to salvation: *annihilation.*

Timeless and without form, I heard Loretta's voice for the last time, reverberating through the twisting tendrils of the abyss. Trembling but doused in ecstasy through intervals of joyful cries.

She kept repeating, "Thank you!"

But I knew that praise wasn't for me, but *The Womb*. Loretta was spared and provided remittance for offering me to the yawning cavity. Her time would come soon enough, too.

Somewhere faint in the swimming chaos, I heard an infant cry.

And my existence—*extinguished.*

HE WHO KNOCK'S 'EM DEAD

I strolled with ease onto the dim lit stage, and despite my anxiety—nothing, a nice cocktail and a few shots didn't fix beforehand—I was able to introduce myself to the silent anticipation of such a hungry crowd. The spotlight flicked on with a harsh snap, engulfing me in a beam of warm light. I could see my sweat shimmering under the glare of the stage lights.

I could see them too.

Out there. Beyond. Obscured by shadows.

I couldn't make out any defining features to separate or single anyone out. To me, the audience—*my audience*—was like a hive working as one unified organism. Seeing, breathing, and thinking together. An assimilation of, not only flesh, but consciousness. My audience watched with salivating mouths. Their nostrils flared rich with fresh pollution. A thousand eyes, all on me. They couldn't wait to laugh.

Back in the good ol' days, comedy was a different kind of joke. The comics were erratic and unpredictable, navigating through their acts with pure anarchy. Running their mouths about their shitty relationships, the shitty world, and doing all kinds of dope. God forbid, they lampoon The Man in their routine. Folks must have gotten sick of that.

Come on!

We all know The Man did.

Those comedians, from top-billed to circus clown, ended up strung up by their tongues in public squares or blowing their brains out after the apologies no longer sufficed to the public.

I saw it happen.

The art of comedy has changed alot since the days of the harlequins. Today we are a most exalted style of court jesting in the apollonian structure.

No more crude tv appearances or street-side miming.

No way!

Yes, things have changed, we are much more refined, cultured; sophisticated if you will, but we still employ props like machetes, rusty razor blades, or any object that inflicts physical pain.Sure it makes it easy to get a great laugh, but it's so much more than that. Our bodies are works of art. As comedians, we are trying to transcend. Exist purely as the performance. Our names, our birthdays, our emotions must be cast aside for the sake of the performance.

And the laughter.

Unfortunately, we are an endangered species. Soon enough there won't be any of us left in The Kastle after we all do our final shows. I guess that's why we still pack them in like rabid hyenas. Outside The Kastle, the world seems to appreciate us as a misplaced catharsis and they come for miles to see us suffer.

This work ain't for everybody. That's for damn sure.

I started this particular routine with a brief discussion of my shackles. They're always clanking behind my ass, I might as well find a way to include the rusty anchors in my act.

"They say that a real comedian needs no props, well then what the hell is this thing?" I shook my chains, and they jingled in my hands until I dropped them with a loud clunk on my foot. I yelped like those old *Tom & Jerry* cartoons. They let us watch the oldies on the tube in the Kastle. I don't know what I'll do for inspiration when that thing burns out. The crowd wasn't buying it, though. It was quieter than a crypt, except decomposition made more noise than this audience.

My heart thumped a bit louder. I could see it pulse under the fabric of my shirt. Just adrenaline. The buzz from my last dose at the bar kept my blood pressure down. It was time for my next gag. The Man hadn't brought in the groomers in a hot minute, so my nails were like a handful of straight razors. I gnawed on them to give them some serrated edge.

"You know folks, I've been in a real need for a manicure." I smiled. My index finger dug deep into the top of my cheekbone and moved down toward my chin. My flesh peeled like the skin from an apple, curling along with the violent stroke. They must have seen something similar to this one because I didn't hear even a lone giggle. Not a gasp or awe. Nothing. But hey, I'm not a magician. The smoke and mirrors shit has been banned for decades anyways. *This is comedy.* Not a child's birthday party. This crowd doesn't want to be insulted with cheap laughs. They want something that will make them think.

I should've listened to the bartender. She was quite the looker, too. The way her scars and burns intersected gave the illusion that her skin was always crawling. I liked that. Her beauty was calming enough, but her words of encouragement really got me in the mood.

I must say the shots didn't hurt my confidence either.

"You're going to knock 'em dead. I can feel it." She squeezed my forearm and tapped my vein. "You have potential, kid, and the audience can sense that. Don't patronize them. They know you got a mound of flesh, plenty of pain, and endless suffering. That's why they are here. A real artist sheds real blood." The needle penetrated my skin and her thumb pressed the plunge on the syringe. The glowing contents emptied into my bloodstream. My eyes rolled and fluttered. She slid another shot of pills in the little cup. "This one is on me." Her dirty finger hit her lips. *Shhh...*

I nodded, but I was afraid to smile at her. You never know who's watching.

"You just got to be creative. Give 'em something unforgettable. The Man never makes mistakes. You got plucked from up there in The Kastle tonight for a reason. Just like a ripe apple. This is your time. You're gonna transcend. I just know it."

Her tongue ran across the red blisters on her top lip and she winked.

"You're right."

I tossed back the chalky yellow ones and chased them with the tingly blue ones. My throat went numb as they slid down my esophagus. I'm not much of a guy for mixing meds, but this wasn't amateur night. I was going to need the oomph.

My face scrunched up as I gulped down the last pill. I opened my eyes, and the bartender was gone. I watched myself drift into the mirror behind the bar. It reminded me of when I used to practice in the reflection of shattered glass in The Kastle. I've been working on this routine for a long time. Practice makes perfect, and I got the scars to prove it.

The reflection zoomed in and out, and the neon logos for Xantrol and Orzak swirled like a tye-dyed vortex. A colorful brightness flooded my vision, the blues and purples formed laughing faces with bulging yellow eyes and bright red noses. The faces eventually dissipated into emptiness. I thought I heard the crowd laughing, but it could easily have been my own chuckles. The side-effects of The Man's regulated meds are funny sometimes.

I was human, and that is what the audience wanted. That's how true art is made; from the fibrous tissue and sinews, the rivulets of blood, the flesh hanging from the bones, and all the black bile that keeps us living. It all keeps art alive and well. Organic.

Somewhere down the line, before The Man, we choked on enough plastic and lies that we said fuck this. Give us something real. Something that bleeds. Something that can die but lives forever in our memory. The audience wants authenticity. The Kastle hasn't produced any failures yet.

Creative. Right. So, let's try this one on for size. The numbness of my bladder could work like a charm, and I had the advantage of wearing the standard-issue grey and white patterned pants from The Kastle. As blood trickled down my cheek, dripping off the hanging meat of my face, my white shirt absorbed the droplets of blood until my right shoulder was pure crimson. That's when I decided to piss myself. The warm wet stain grew from a small spot on my crotch down my left leg. I danced like a marionette across the stage. Adopting some moves I had seen from puppet shows on the tube.

It was the big one, I thought. They will die laughing.

Yet, it was silent. I would have been more nervous, but those shots were still going strong. Xantrol and Orzak were a powerful combination. I couldn't feel a thing, and I questioned if all this was some vivid hallucination.

The spotlight shone against my skin, and I could feel its warmth from across the venue. The emergency exit in the back trailed in my vision while I swayed like dandelion pappus whisked away in the wind. Carry me to a place with roaring laughter louder than thunderheads on a black ocean.

Raw meat shredded between their teeth. Bloody sloshing in their cheeks and smacking lips emanated from below the front of the stage. The audience was not impressed. They were hungry.

Trust in The Man.

I grabbed the microphone from its stand as a warrior would a saber from a sheath and held it up high in the illumination of the stage. My weapon. My salvation. I slammed it into my forehead. My skull started to cave in. The cracking fragments of my noggin amplified in between the shrill of squealing feedback.

"Hot mike!" I shouted.

Only one eye was working, there was a ringing in my ear, and it wasn't the feedback. My fingers felt the empty, spongy cavity where my right eye used to be. A string of wet tendons hung from the orifice and connected to a jelly-like sphere. I lifted my hanging eyeball and turned it toward myself. My mangled face flashed back a crooked smile.

"Talk about a sight for sore eyes, eh?" I laughed at my joke.

But the audience stood unamused.

I squeezed my hanging eyeball until it popped and oozed into an amorphous blob running down my wrist. "You could put an eye out with this thing." Broken teeth spit out and tic-tacked as they landed on the wooden flooring of the stage.

Silence in the darkness beyond the stage lights.

I wondered why I wanted to be a comedian, but I remembered I never had a choice. In The Kastle, I often daydreamed of laughter and happiness, but I knew there was only laughter and suffering. It never hurts to pretend. My eyes were always closed, even in pure darkness, and the imagined laughter created soothing melodies. In between each echoing crack of the whip, between each newly formed scar, I heard a roar of laughter. I felt it! My tears were smiles. Tragedy is pure comedic gold.

I couldn't give up. I had a duty, a service to provide. I had no choice.

Pain and suffering: my god. They must laugh or die.

A memory struck me. When The Man let loose, I was on a date at the public execution, and I was hoping to get a kiss from him, but the criminal standing before the crowd stole my attention. He was one of those starving artists. Hunger artist they used to call them. The hunger artists spent weeks at a time withering away to nothing in the streets. Naked and cold, the closest thing you could get to a corpse without being dead. They were the real pioneers of the work us comedians do today.

You could play the xylophone on the hunger artist's ribcage. The rope around his neck had rubbed his pallid skin red and raw like a necklace of strawberries, but he smiled at the crowd and said his final words, "to die laughing must be the most glorious of all deaths." The floor dropped beneath him and there he went. His neck cracked, disrupting the quiet crowd. His body swung limp a few times like a pendulum until the hooded executioner cut him down. As the executioner lifted his body, I noticed he was still smiling. Others must have noticed because after a few giggles, the whole assembly belted out gut-busting laughter. Then an awful riot broke out. One of the worst in our history. Trust me, I was there through the whole thing.

The Man let the beasts loose. Limbs were torn and shredded by the gnashing fangs. The dismemberment piled in the puddles of blood in the streets and asphalt was stained red. The whole city started to burn into an inferno, so The

Man sent in the firing squad. Machine guns leveled the mass of bodies down. I watched heads explode as the bullets ripped through the frenzy of violence. Any survivors left in the ash and rubble after the night of chaos still laughing got thrown up into The Kastle. *Welcome home*, they said.

Haha. I can't help but laugh thinking about it all. I was inspired that day. I was changed. Reborn into the person that I am now and there was no going back.

They told us The Man did what they did for the greater good. To restore faith in unity and order. Our society fell from grace and they saved us from decadence and self-destruction. I don't know about all that. Of course, I would never speak my thoughts of such contempt. I couldn't stop thinking of the hunger artist's posthumous smile. And I do know I had a purpose.

I gave them all I had. My closing monologue. The final bow.

Cold stares from a thousand eyes, and each blinked and winked out of sync with their brothers and sisters. Large bulging pupils protruded from the other clusters of beady peepers peering at my performance. Those cold stares pierced right through me like icicles. The possessors of those eyes must have missed the punchline.

The stage lights might as well have been a dying star and I was on a planet orbiting death. The good thing about the coming darkness was that it obscured the world staring back at you. The light eclipsing dark. The worlds apart. The thin veil between spectators and the spectacle. Who is who?

These vapid thoughts don't mean much. At this point, nothing meant much. I was a nameless shape, a broken mannequin standing still under a dimming spotlight. Soon to be only a silhouette of a person. Perhaps, I was always only a contour to them.

My thoughts began to lose form, the words in them vanishing in definition until I was the purest form of suffering.

Nothing could hide their eyes. Those never seemed to fade. If hell exists, it's up here on stage. *Welcome home*, they said.

One shadowy abomination waited to laugh, except there were no coughs or chirping crickets heard in the stillness of this place. Nothing.

Tough crowd, I thought, that last joke went way over their heads.

The lights went out.

Maybe, I'll give 'em a minute. But I couldn't stop laughing.

NEED A LIGHT?

His Doc Martens tracked trails of muddy footprints throughout the trailer. Steve tossed his worn-out leather jacket over the back of the couch. It reeked of gas fumes—either from huffing or his puddering '83 Pontiac Firebird he named Eva. Bare arms revealed a collective of jailhouse tattoos. Crooked swastikas and scribbled SS emblems decorated his mayonnaise flesh from his legs to his bald head. He claimed he was stopping by to *burn one* but instead preached on the horrors of miscegenation into Tara's wrinkled mug.

"I got locked up with a guy that got a *sista* pregnant," he said, holding in a deep hit.

"Hmm?" Tara's cigarette ash was longer than her press-on nails. She didn't even feel the ember blistering her fingers. She nodded in and out of a dope coma, meeting coherence each time.

"Real ugly thing. The doctors even said they should've put it out of its misery," Steve said.

Steve's grin could shred aluminum cans. The only thing

that made him happier than his racial tangents was making Ren's life a living hell.

Ren tip-toed past the living room, but their trailer was no bigger than a cracker box. You couldn't take a shit without stinking up the whole place.

"Ren," Steve shouted just as he turned the doorknob to his room. "You been hanging out with that nigger? Lucky you faggots can't reproduce, right Tara?" Steve choked up laughing; billows of smoke drifted from his sordid jaw.

"I don't know, man. I'm just wondering how you manage to always look like a used condom." Ren winked, although he knew he had just fucked himself. *Here we go again,* he thought.

"If I wasn't fucking your mom, I'd curb stomp the braces off them teeth." A long drag off the joint, and he stuffed it in the ashtray.

"Fuck off, Steve. That skinhead shit is a front. We all know you took it up the ass in prison."

Crimson soaked up Steve's pale muzzle. He launched at Ren from the couch and they crashed through the front door. Ren bolted, but the boots stomped with thunder. Each tread gained momentum, until two tattooed paws gripped Ren's shirt, yanking him down into the sod. A mouthful of dirt and a few blades of grass short of a pile of dog shit, Ren thought this might be the day he eats it. Steve's boot pressed hard against Ren's cheek and clumps of soil pushed from his mouth.

"Damnit, Steven. Don't hurt him again. You know how nosy the goddamn neighbors are. Y'all are going to wake up the whole damn trailer park. I don't want to deal with no fucking cops tonight," Tara shouted. "Sniffin' around with search warrants and poppin' your trunk."

"Shut the fuck up, Tara!" Steve snapped. "If anything's gonna wake somebody up, it's your mouth."

Steve reached out his hand in a gesture of mercy, but as Ren gripped, he was lunged forward. Steve's foot became a hammer. The blow cracked into his ribcage, elevating him several feet. His abdomen wrapped around the boot, vaporizing his breath. Ren's limp body thwacked the ground like a scene from Tom & Jerry. The cartoonish onomatopoeias rippled behind Steve's loom. Ren hunkered over, holding back vomit, but still gulped to regain his breath. The dim stars circled his head, dissipating while oxygen returned to his lungs.

Steve craned down and whispered, "next time, I'll fucking kill you."

He strutted across the yard to Tara with a cigarette dangling from his lips. He pinched her ass and she released a coy giggle. Steve turned back to Ren beaming his jagged smile of rot and decay. "And keep your fucking bike away from Eva! If you scratch the paint job on my car, that promise will come sooner than later." His boot hiked up and knocked over Ren's bike. "If you weren't such a pussy, I might show you some stuff I got in the trunk that'll make you sprout some hairs on your balls."

Ren limped back to the couch and slumped into the frayed cushions. He thumbed through a xeroxed pamphlet laid on the table. *STAND UNITED* never explicitly stated any affiliation, but he took the hint from the iron crosses on the cover and the hefty use of the term *pureblood* that they weren't the local Moose Lodge.

The theme song from *Cops* blared from inside the main bedroom. Laughter along with the smell of burnt plastic seeped from beneath the locked door. Regardless of his time spent in prison for amphetamines, Steve was not ashamed to admit he loved to smoke meth.

"These neanderthals keep the damn pigs in business." Steve hacked between words. "Woohoo! I bet we can go at it for hours tonight, baby."

Muffled voices quieted along with the muted volume. Awful rhythmic squeaking accelerated with heavy thumps whose epicenter was concealed by the bedroom's walls. Soft moans and brash ape-like grunts insinuated the signal to exit. In his painful attempt to leap from the couch, Ren noticed something on the coffee table.

A barely-smoked joint laid in the ashtray. Steve seemed to have forgotten all about it while knocking Ren's insides into jelly. *Easy mistake.* Ren picked up the hog's leg, contemplating trying it out. His mom seemed to enjoy the stuff, and he'd always heard of being high as this fantastic voyage of psychedelia. Plus, he thought maybe it would ease the throbbing pain in his side. *I wonder what Vic will think?* Ren thought.

He shot out the front door and lifted his bike off the ground. As he rolled by *Eva*, preparing to ride off, he braked just before hitting the gravel of his street. Ren stared at the carousel paint job and heard Steve's voice repeating, *next time I'll fucking kill you.*

Ren dug his house key into the hood, dragging it across with a pleasing screech. Flecks of red paint fluttered in the air like glitter. It reminded him of a birthday party he had a long time ago at Buggy Burger KidZone. This was before his mom was strung out and his dad ran off with "that hooker" as Tara always put it. It was one of his last good memories, framed in a polaroid in a cluttered kitchen drawer, still sparkling with glittery residue from the party.

He grinned.

Ren felt the scratches continue grinding away, vibrating the bones in his fingers. The key dug deeper as he reflected on all the *good times* with Skinhead Steve. Ren hated hearing the car's name, but he hoped Steve screamed "Eva!" once he saw the piece of shit carved up worse than his bad tattoos. *Go ahead, fucking kill me. It's the only way to get rid of you!*

THE TAPPING at the window roused Victor from his nightly routine of horror movies and junk food. He was ravaging through a bag of hot fries when he heard a familiar call through the glass. "Victor! Open up!" Ren waved his hands by his bicycle shrouded in a crepuscular mist.

The window slid up, and Victor's head poked out fashioned for a fast-food drive-thru. "God, do you smell that skunk?" His face scrunched up. "Man, what happened to you, Steve kick your ass again?"

Ren, still spotted with grass stains and dirt, pulled the joint from his t-shirt pocket.

"What's that?" Victor retreated to his turtle shell.

"A joint."

"Is that your Mom's?"

"Steve's."

"I'll pass. It could be angel dust."

"It's just a joint. I promise—well, I hope."

"No way. My parents will kill me, and if they find out I'm smoking pot with you, they will never let us hang out again. They already don't like me going over there, thanks to Steve." Victor shook his head.

"Come on. It's our last summer before high school. We cannot go in a couple of pussies. They will eat us alive."

Candy wrappers and the stack of overdue tapes rented from Monster Video littered the bed. It defined their entire summer. Victor suddenly realized he spent most of his time talking shit and ogling playboy centerfolds with Ren. Not once thinking about the transition into high school.

"Okay, okay. We absolutely cannot smoke it here, though, so where did you have in mind?"

"Happy Ridge."

"Happy Ridge?" Victor shuddered.

"You don't believe all that crazy shit about UFOs and devil worshippers or whatever? Unsolved Mysteries is warping your mind. That's little kid shit, Vic."

"I guess not."

"We'll be fine unless you want to be a little bitch and go watch Terminator 2 for the eight hundredth time."

"Goddamnit, okay. I'll be right down.

"Victor?"

"Yeah?"

"Bring a lighter."

Bicycles glided over freshly paved asphalt, interloping between the parallel yellow lines that ran down the middle of the street. The cicadas chirped a summer melody as they wound around curves that seemed to yield into more intricate contortions the closer they got to Happy Ridge. The lonely road running up the hillside to their destination finally veered off into a single gravel path lined by giant gray boulders.

Flickering street lights departed, leaving the lone luminosity of a trillion blinking stars and the pale moon's gaze. The canopy of the cosmos radiated a sapphire hue upon the black Earth, and in limited sight, scattered the contours of many-limbed trees and massive boulders protruding from the crude nightscape like a graveless cemetery. They followed the gravel path across the gulf of frolicking shadows until halting at a mossy rock formation.

"Lighter, Victor."

"Here." Victor pulled out a small book of matches.

"Matches?"

"My mom always lights one after she takes a shit, so I just snatched them from the bathroom." Ren rolled his eyes along with a frustrated sigh. "This was *your* idea. Why didn't you bring a lighter? Your mom's the crackhead," Victor said.

"Methhead, asshole. Whatever, fire is fire, hand them over."

Ren struck the first match against the burgundy patch; a pathetic spark twinkled before exhausting.

"Dud. Let me try again." After several tries, finally, a flare burst into a trembling flame. The match's irradiation trailed to the joint and began to cherry until a light breeze extinguished their plan.

"Fuck! Seriously? That was the last match." Ren growled.

"Oh well, it just wasn't meant to be. Let's go home. I bet it's not too late to rent a video. We can watch *Ace Ventura* instead of *T2* since you're so fucking sick of it."

Ren's silence was a prayer for fire.

Silence listened.

"Hey, you boys need a light?" A bodiless voice pervaded the umbra followed by a hacky smoker's cough.

They trembled as the shadowy shape materialized before them.

"Shit. Who said that?" Ren asked.

"You boys need a light?" The silhouette brightened up from a burst of fire, revealing a fleshy, liver spotted hand. Fingers bloomed from the floating fist uncovering a dancing flame in the palm. "Here you go, kid."

"Sir?" Ren puzzled at the flame's source.

"Jim." A voice timeworn and raspy suggested years of unknown suffering.

"Jim, I know you're not a cop. They never come up here unless it's the senior's graduation party. How did you do that fire trick?"

"Shitfire. I ain't no pig. And that was just a little magic."

"Where did you come from?"

"My truck over there." He pointed to a shadowy blob in the distance.

"Easy to miss on the dark side of the moon," Ren said.

"Hell, I been there and this ain't even close, but it sure is dark."

The flame kissed the joint, and Jim clapped his hands, smothering the flame.

Ren took the first hit. His lungs filled with heat, and a pillar of smoke poured from his mouth like a dying dragon. Kneeled over in a coughing fit, his hand popped up to pass it along. Victor pinched the joint and followed in line.

"So, what are you doing up here, Jim?" Victor asked.

"Drinkin' and thinkin'."

Victor's coughs didn't match the intensity of Ren's, but he still wheezed alongside him.

"I take it you boys ain't big dope smokers?"

Instead of answering, Victor handed over the joint. Jim inhaled deeply, and the burning cherry cast a tangerine glow against his lips. Most of his face, obscured by darkness, yet a single eye peeked through dissipating smoke. He barked up some phlegmy coughs and handed the joint back to Ren.

"How about a beer, boys? Cheap shit, but I'm sure y'all don't mind. We're gonna need something for this cotton-mouth." Jim ushered them with a flashlight. Stepping over patches of grass and twigs, they continued to pass the joint. A Chevy pickup sat parked by a dead tree. The windows were rolled down and rust had eaten most of the sky blue paint away except for a few spots around the chrome bumpers and truck bed.

"You feel anything, Ren?"

Vic's eyes look like baboon ass cheeks, Ren thought.

A minute passed before he actually responded.

"I think so." Ren chuckled as he leaned up against the rusted side of the truck. His vision—lucid and crisp—tinged with colorful vibrancy. The sky seemed more kinetic. The light tufts of clouds curled as they were carried away by a nocturnal breeze. Ren noticed the gooseflesh on Victor's arms.

"What about you?"

Their faint classroom giggles matured to the cackling of hyenas. The echoes of their laughter swelled through the terrain, resonating in the vacancy.

Jim opened up a cooler in the bed of his truck, shuffling through icy water. His hands emerged with dripping cans of Shooster's Ice. "Here you go, boys." Two beers tumbled through the air waiting for a catch. Victor was slow to react. The beer aimed for him slipped his grip.

"Be careful with that one, kid," Jim said.

Victor and Ren didn't drink—ever—but didn't want to seem like wimps. Two snaps synced, and the cans tipped upward. The frothy gulp slugged cold down their throats and they exchanged sour looks.

"I know you boys ain't old enough to drink," Jim said.

"We're fourteen. You?" Victor said.

"Old." Jim left it at that. "I know what you're thinkin', boys. I ain't some molester. For so long I've been alone and to be honest with you, I was coming up here to put a bullet in my brain."

Responses drifted in the gravity of such heavy information, but amid a long awkward silence, a stoned Ren said the only thing that came to mind. "Don't do it, Jim."

"Death ain't the worst to come." Jim tipped the can up, crushed it in his fist, and tossed it into the bordering abyss. "I tell you what. You boys want to see some wild shit?"

Jim yanked open his truck door and fiddled for a minute until the motor rumbled. The ignition flipped while the exhaust spat a surge of metallic putters until finally turning over with a roar. "This Ain't the Summer of Love" by Blue Oyster Cult exploded from the stereo, and the headlights flooded the area with brightness. Jim bobbed and jigged as he sloshed around the cooler for more beers. "You're going to need another cold one for this shit."

Leaning over the hood of the car, Jim struggled for the courage to reveal his secret, muttering inaudible phrases to himself. Victor gaped at Ren and nodded his head in the opposite direction. He mouthed, *let's fucking go!* Conspiring paranoia corrupted their thoughts, roving a scenario where they were mutilated or murdered in such a vile, unspeakable manner. They were certain to be the next ghost story collected in the heinous history of Happy Ridge.

"It's getting late. I think Vic and I are heading home, Jim. Thanks for the beers."

Jim wrenched into the beams of the headlights, revealing a putrid spectacle. Ren and Victor were uncertain if what they were looking at could be considered a *face*.

"You guys are my only friends, and I figured I should be honest with y'all."

The barnacle-like growths and decaying flesh writhed from his neck to his balding crown of stringy grey hair. A bulging, yellow eye sunk in folds of the squirming tissue. It blinked and dripped with puss. The malignant mask was a blasphemous imitation of the human image.

"Jim, no offense, but I think you might need to see a doctor." Victor's voice fumbled.

"No doctor could fix this. If they looked too close, they'd go looney."

"No shit," Ren blurted out before Victor nudged his bruised ribs. "I mean, there has to be another way out, right?"

"Kid, you don't want to know what I know. " Jim chuckled as he pulled a cigarette pack from a frayed pocket of his faded blue jeans.

"Can't be that bad, right?" Ren shrugged him off but shuddered inside.

"Trust me on this. You don't want to know. Stick to heaven and hell. Less questions, the better." That time with more certainty.

"Try us."

"I couldn't even say after floating between all that purple haze. And all them empty spots between the skeletons and other cosmic muck up there; I been dead. Like I said, it ain't the worst of it." He pointed to the sky with a cigarette between his fingers. "It's too much for a simple mind like myself to describe, but those things shrieked in the blackness while I floated around, and I've seen things fuck, that shouldn't have the parts to fuck each other. I don't ever want to have to go through that shit again.

"Then something puked me up like it was a bad hangover and the last thing I remember real clearly—as Jim—is since I got this." Jim's arm swung behind his hip and pulled out an old revolver that reminded Ren of something he'd seen from a western. "This is Peacemaker. Got it from a man they called Judge out west. I was selling Indian scalps, then business slowed down, and I drifted east. Worked some sideshows, some circuses, as a maimed magician. I always tended to fuck up. Doing something real awful. Folks end up hurt. I either get left behind or have to be on the run. And I've always been alone. Might as well have been another nameless thing shrieking in the blackness beyond Mgo."

The volume of his words fell silent while staring into the sky. He hung his head down and examined his revolver, gently touching the barrel with his fingers.

"Peacemaker, I always like the sound of it, and I was hoping the namesake was right. Lord knows I need it." He carelessly clicked through the chamber and cocked the hammer. The revolver gravitated to his temple, and his finger squeezed.

"No!" They shouted and waved their hands.

The revolver clicked short of a flag that read *bang!* Jim laughed and slapped his knee. "I'll tell you what. Life'll getcha sometimes."

Their mouths both agape and speechless, Ren cocked his head, attempting to comprehend Jim's presence as real or imaginary, or something beyond.

A resonant metallic roared behind them. The pale vista of Happy Ridge blossomed with two amber orbs barrelling through the blanket of moonshine.

"Shit," Ren said. "Jim, it was nice knowing you, but we have to go."

"Fuck. It's the cops, isn't it?" Victor panicked. "My mom is going to kill me."

"Worse," Ren said. "I don't know how he found me, but he did."

"He was going to find you sooner or later. Doesn't matter much now, does it?" The barrel of the gun slid down the front of Jim's worn-out jeans, and he strode forward from his truck. "Don't worry, boys. I got your backs. Peacemaker will make due."

The boys were too concerned with impending doom from the approaching storm.

Eva cut a hard turn around a boulder, breaking just in front of their congregation. The car door slammed shut, and Steve exited from a swirling cloud of dirt. He dusted off and flashed his signature razor-wire grin. The headlights from both vehicles shined on the perfect stage for a standoff.

"He's pissed. What did you do?" Victor asked.

"Did you happen to check out the new paint job on the Trans Am?" Ren's eyebrows raised.

A crude carving abraded across the front of the car with jagged intersecting lines running down the entire paint job.

"Harsh, Ren, even for this piece of shit."

"Are you kidding? He almost made my face worse than Jim's." Ren turned to Jim. "Sorry, Jim. No offense."

"None taken, partner."

Violence clenched in Steve's fists. "You couldn't have picked a better spot for me to kill you. You thought you were going to get away with this? You thought you were going to come up here to Queer Lovers' Lane and get away with fucking up Eva and stealing my stash?" Steve marched until he stopped at Jim and grimaced. "Who's this fucking mutant?"

"Name's Jim." Absent of fear, Jim extended his hand.

Steve craned his mug in Jim's face. "You get kicked out the fucking carnival?" Steve reared his head back and hawked a juicy loogie into Jim's face. "Get the fuck out of my way."

Steve's lips split showing each broken and rotten tooth, exposing the green crud on his gums. Steve's head flew back, laughing with hateful ecstasy. "You freaks can share a fucking grave together. Put your fucking teeth on—"

Interrupted by the flash and sonic boom, Steve's final words were cut short as his body flopped to the ground.

Ren and Victor covered their ears and crouched in one motion. Their ears rang once they rose from their huddle. Steve's head hosted an oozing exit wound of brain matter and gore.

Jim's one visible eye winked behind a smoking gun barrel.

Speechless amidst the night's newborn secret. The lifeless body of Skinhead Steve laid in a shallow grave of puddling blood and dirt.

"Shitfire boys, I thought I was going to be digging my own grave tonight." Jim smiled. "Don't you kids worry. I'll take care of this."

They stood there for a moment, reveling in the intensity of what trauma they experienced. Ren felt he needed to say something. Anything, but he could only utter one thing, "thanks, Jim."

"No need to thank me. I ain't worth it."

Without hesitation, they rode off beneath a swallowing sky. Shadows galloped at their side in majestic strides, and the wind's howl faded to a whisper of secrets. Ren looked back and witnessed something that made him want to hollow out his eye sockets. In the hazy beams from the car was something not of this world. An image he never wanted to remember. He was relieved as he drifted away to be as far away from whatever he saw happening. The car's headlights went dim like starlight devoured by darkness.

THE NINETIES SLITHERED by like slugs, each one trailing with vapid memories. Sometime in those passing years, a fisherman out on the Ohio River got their lines stuck on Steve's car and called it in. State Police got involved and discovered a trunk full of kiddie porn. No body was discovered, but by that time, the memory of Steve was a mental discharge in everybody's mind and his disappearance was not a high priority.

That was it.

Case closed.

The entire town certainly was happy to be rid of Skinhead Steve regardless of any disturbing details. Tara moved on to the next piece of shit without so much as a tear. She assumed he ran off on a meth-fueled bender or finally said the wrong thing in the wrong place.

The dull edge of life was uninspired after that night.

Nintendo and horror flicks from Monster Video kept Ren occupied while Victor tended to focus on more educational interests. High school didn't drift them apart despite their differing academic commitments. How could it? Their friendship forever bonded by the ineffable.

Each year's monotony was an imitation of fulfillment. Making the honor roll and getting your driver's license were disguised as joy. Victor's mom insisted that hard work kept the boys out of trouble. That might work for some kids, but for them, it helped them forget that strange summer night.

As with every graduating class, a bonfire was held at Happy Ridge to celebrate the class of '99 as a rite of passage. The blazing fire painted the darkness with shimmering gold while the people danced around it like a witches' sabbath. Beer foamed over red plastic cups, and a haze of smoke drifted between clusters of drunkenness. They indulged in the pleasure and freedom of entering adulthood and discussed the future like it was already in their grasps.

After the inferno diminished to dwindling flames, the glassy-eyed graduates dispersed. Ren rested by a dead tree that felt all too familiar. Victor walked over, patted him on the back, and swigged from a bottle of Kessler before passing it.

"Can I ask you something? Something I've been wanting to ask for a while now."

"What?" Ren gulped his shot of cheap whiskey like lighter fluid.

"What the fuck happened *that night*?"

Ren paused and took another shot before handing it back to Victor. *That night?* Ren thought, but he couldn't lie to himself. "I thought I had forgotten about it. If I did remember anything, I just assumed it was a fucked up dream."

"I didn't even want to come tonight, I don't know why. It just happened. Then when I got here I remembered Steve's fucking brains," Victor fumbled his words and a tear dripped from one eye. "And that face. I guess I feel guilt. I don't really know how I feel about it. Steve was a fucking prick, maybe he deserved it and—"

"Is all that worth remembering?" Ren interrupted. "Let those memories burn out like this match." He plucked the final match from a pack he pulled from his back pocket and stared at it.

"Wonder what happened to him?"

"Who?" Ren asked. His focus, still on the match.

"Jim."

"Gotta be dead."

But what if he wasn't? Ren thought.

Somewhere behind them, a car stereo blasted a palm-muted guitar riff before kicking into a melody that stained the chasm of their fragmented memories. They passed the bottle a few more times, listening to "It Ain't The Summer of Love" and staring at the dimming landscape. Victor suggested they leave before the bonfire burns out and the cops show up to break up the party. Ren told him to wait for him in the car while he puffs down a cig.

His gaze turned to the stars, watching the clusters of twinkling stars blackout, one by one devoured by darkness. That awful sight snapped back into his brain. The memory rose goosebumps up his arms. He *needed* a smoke.

He pulled out a cigarette, attempting to light the end with his last match, but a breeze blew out the flame.

"Shit," Ren said.

Behind him he heard a familiar voice. "Need a light?"

NECROZOIC

Ezra arrived prepared for the uproar. Just as he darted up the rickety, wooden staircase that ascended the only entrance to the garage apartment, the fucking dog starts barking and howling. Never fails, Ezra thought. The day Trixie defies domestication and finally rips my leg off.

"Trixie, you bitch! Get on back here, girl," Ranch hollered with a mouthful of long-cut tobacco. Trixie regressed back to man's best friend, and pranced to Ranch's side, just a few inches from his other best friend: his gun. "You tell that loony friend of yours the rents due!"

"You got it, Ranch," Ezra said.

"Oh, and tell him to keep that goddamn devil music down," Ranch hawked a wad of brownish-yellow spit.

The floodlight flickered and hummed above the doorway, illuminating the porch that seemed to levitate in the black rural stillness. Thousands of tiny insects swarmed the spiderwebs hanging in each nook. Ezra swatted any bit of exposed flesh the moment he stepped on the porch. The door opened for him, and Graham awaited.

"God damn, that dog never shuts up. I have something to drown that hollering out," Graham said.

"Yeah, get anything cool? By the way, you desperately need a bug zapper. These things are out of control."

"Fuck those bugs."

Graham's collection always had new additions, whether it be a tape, vinyl record, or even better: a zine. They were like a couple of kids peeking at pornos before the internet.

These possessions came to define Graham. He was never hot shit in high school, and one incident with a parking cone emasculated him. Graham spent hours meticulously combing through his infinite wardrobe of rare Black Metal t-shirts while flexing in the mirror. He was determined to be the most elite— at all costs.

"The postal dude has to be sick of this route by now," Graham laughed. "Here's some new hits for you, Ez. I can't even pronounce most of this shit, but check this out, too."

Graham picked up a crinkled black and white cluster of papers and slapped it on the coffee table.

Ezra gulped his beer and crushed the can in his fist. The garbage overflowed with empty bottles and cans. Graham chucked another full one to Ezra, and he popped the tab in one swift motion like an alley-oop.

"Where's this one from?!" Ezra shouted over the ear-splitting music.

"I honestly don't remember ordering it."

The cover depicted a timeworn gravesite surrounded by knots of rotting vegetation. Vines slithered up massive bone monoliths from beneath a ground of black foliage. Black blurs formed like shadowy vultures looming atop the sinister structure. The image appeared prehistoric, maybe older. *What is older than that?* Ezra thought. He murmured the inscription at the top of the zine, "Necrozoic."

Graham lumbered across the living room into the hallway. He entered the spare room he christened, *The Evil Room*, a hive of black metal paraphernalia. The door snapped, and immediately, the volume rose to a clarion screech. Graham ran down the hallway holding his black baseball bat, playing air guitar. He claimed the bat was for protection but so far had only served as a prop for his corpse paint photos. The bat cut the air with light swishes as he grinned.

"Get the fuck up! You have to listen to this. *Real darkness*, man. This shit will block out the sun!"

Ezra gulped down a big swig of shitty beer and thought about *real darkness*. Was this a concept they wanted to invoke or was it the same buzz you get from a horror flick?

"Who is this?"

"Vornat," Graham slightly bobbed his head with a crooked smile.

"Cornut?" Ezra heard him, but he liked to fuck with Graham on his high horse. They laughed and continued to slam beer while the loud music continued.

Ezra flipped through Necrozoic and inspected the tape trading list: J. Holocaust of Berlin, Gaad from Poland; the list traversed through a few more tape-dubbing elitists until at the bottom was the contact info for the creator, followed by an abstruse edict.

FOR FURTHER CONSPIRACY CONTACT

AL
AL@necrozoic.com
SERIOUS INQUIRIES ONLY!!!!!

THE GEOLOGIC TIME SCALE ABUSED BY
HUMANKIND AND THEIR DENIAL CANNOT

CONTINUE. REASSEMBLED SKELETONS ERECTED IN
ERROR, FALSE FOSSILS, AND CLADISTIC
HYPOTHESIS ASSUMED IN ARROGANCE. FUCK
JURASSIC PARK AND THE CORRUPT
CORPORATIONS THAT ATTEMPT TO DEPRECIATE
THE SINGULARITY OF THE TRUE EARTH
AGE. THE DAY THE OF THE CRATER WILL BE A
FUCKING DUMPSTER. GLOBAL
HAIL EXTINCTION! HAIL THE MILLENNIUM OF
REAL DARKNESS!

"Graham, this guy is off his fucking rocker."

"Really?"

"Yeah, his email is here. Serious inquiries only and some conspiracy harangue."

"He's just trying to be scary. Let's inquire."

Ezra woke up gasping for air as his phone vibrated under his pillow.

"Fuck," he taps the answer button. "Hello?"

"Ezra!"

"Yes, Graham? You realize what time it is?"

It was not unusual for Graham to spontaneously call Ezra at odd hours of the night. His voice charged with energy in comparison to his usual speaking voice.

"Dude, I have something for you. Come over!"

"Sure, I will tonight, but I have to get some fucking sleep first."

"No, now. Come over now. AL sent me a tape. I think you need to see," Graham paused. "I mean, hear."

"I don't think I can handle the tape fuzz right now."

"It is so much more than that. Please."

Maybe Graham sniffed cocaine or took too much Adderall? Ezra worried that he needed supervision, as he was not known for his wise-decision making skills. Graham once ate a bunch of mushrooms and claimed he could walk up walls.

"So, are you coming?" Graham asked after an extended silence.

"Goddamnit. Yeah, man. I'll be right over." If he didn't, the poor guy might fall up instead of down.

"Ezra?"

"Yeah?"

"AL was right," the call disconnected.

EZRA GRIPPED the railing and felt a slimy substance. His hand jolted back, disgusted by the unforeseen texture. A phosphorescent mold consumed the entire frame of the staircase and porch. The spider webs that once strobed under the porch light's usual flicker now radiated with a strange spectrum of colors.

A radish-colored crustacean claw enveloped in prickly black hairs reached from shadows about the apartment door. The molting exoskeleton revealed itself as a gigantic arachnid with oozing fangs.

The apartment door swung open, and Ezra fell back into a trash bag full of beer cans. The arachnid swiftly retracted up into the shadows, and Ezra's gaze shifted to the doorway. Shimmers of spores danced in the light. He looked back down the mold-covered staircase and contemplated exiting, but

Ranch and Trixie were standing at the bottom in the gloom of the night without their heads.

The mold quickly consumed their headless bodies before Ezra's eyes. He watched in awe until their bodies were devoured by the mold, encasing them in a glowing egg-like cocoon.

"Hey, Ez," Graham stood in the doorway. "What's the matter?"

Ezra glanced around his surroundings and realized that it appeared *normal*. "Just tired as hell," attempting not to seem like the crazy one. "It's the middle of the night, and *you* asked *me* to come over."

"Yeah, so come on in and don't be a dick."

"This better be good. Where's your landlord and that barking demon?" Ezra's way of double-checking his sanity. "Didn't hear when I came up?"

"Vacation. Why do you think the volume is at full blast?"

Graham plopped into his worn-out leather recliner and rocked back and forth for a few minutes with his eyes closed and a disturbing half-grin. Ezra waited for the big reveal and finally broke the silence, "well?"

"Before I show you this, you have to promise to keep an open mind, okay?"

"Just let me listen to the tape so I can go home."

"Okay, give me a minute," Graham rose from his recliner, took a few steps back into the hallway, halted, and turned back, "See anything weird when you came up?"

"No," Ezra's face dropped into a blank stare. "Why?"

"No reason, I was just playing music loud. I didn't want to piss off Ranch's old ass."

"What happened to vacation?"

"Oh yeah, that's right," he continued into the dim-lit hallway and vanished into the shadows of *The Evil Room*.

Ezra paced across the living room, trying to make sense of what was happening. The thought of guzzling a cold beer eased his nerves, so he walked into the tiny kitchen. The refrigerator opened, and Ezra grabbed a beer. He slammed it and let out a loud belch. He reached for another and noticed the puddle of blood coagulating in the cool air. Resting in crimson was the decapitated head of Trixie.

Steam drifted off the top of her head as her tongue hung from her open jaws. Tufts of golden fur crusted in red stains scattered across the bottom with glowing green mold. The decapitated gaze made that beer useless.

Trixie's head growled and dripped red globules from its snarling snout. Ezra slammed the refrigerator shut and sprinted back to the living room. Graham had not returned, and Ezra thought of a brilliant plan: *Get the fuck out of there!*

EZRA LURCHED to the front door. As he passed by the coffee table, he noticed an opened yellow bubble mailer. He dumped out the contents, and a cluster of polaroids scattered across the table.

Bright mushroom caps and glowing mold engulfed rotting corpses and roadkill. Decapitated heads of house pets like cats, birds, and dogs, including one of Trixie, were lined in a row. One of these heads was a human and unmistakably the severed head of Graham's landlord, Ranch.

There were also photographs of towering scaled beasts with pointed teeth, claws, and long tails. Some of them had horns between their eyes, some of them with spines, and some of them were bipedal. Some had translucent membraned wings, and others had nearly a thousand eyes. These things were far from what Ezra remembered learning about in school.

"This doesn't make any fucking sense," Ezra said.

Aside from this spectacle of horrors, one photograph was alluring. A naked man stood beside a massive, moldy egg, and his body covered in bleeding lacerations up to an unkempt brown beard. A large nose bridged into a thick, hairy unibrow resembling a neanderthal. Two glowing yellow eyes peer back at Ezra, along with a smile of broken, rotten teeth.

"Ezra?" Graham caught him before he could walk out the door.

"Graham, what the fuck is going on?" Ezra eased away from polaroids and walked backward toward the door.

"I wanted you to listen to this tape."

"Fine, just make this psychedelic prehistoric shit stop."

"Stop? But it is the ultimate obscure find. AL chose me, man. It tops all of the shirts, tapes, records, and anything else those posers put out. The church-burning pussies have nothing on this shit. Beyond any dark art," Graham started to stutter and tremble. "Th-this is primal; from the rocks that make up this earth. In the dirt, man. Dig in the fucking dirt with me."

Graham's eyes brimmed with tears as he approached Ezra with a portable stereo covered in green mold. It inched closer to his face, and Graham pressed play. The speakers blared out ear-piercing screeches and thundering roars of inhuman frequencies. It was obvious they were never meant to be heard by the human ear.

The door swung open from a powerful gust. Colorful streaks rippled through the air vibrating the fabric of reality. The ripples wrested into gashes that tore into a gaping portal peering into another world.

Reptilian behemoths stomped among a lush garden of exotic vegetation. The horizon burned with an orange, fiery radiance with silhouetted pterodactyls soaring before a raging sun. The behemoths plodded among the forbidden land forming into line as if it were a ritual. Their moaning vocalizations created a melody while forming a circular barrier around a gigantic black monolith protruding from the ground.

These monstrous creatures were unlike skeletal remains in museums or depicted in books. No, they were something indescribable in their mass and never meant to be seen by human eyes.

Although Ezra did not understand their extinct language, he could sense their discontent and envy.

They knew he was watching from the other end of time. It was all part of the ritual. Their song reached a valorous crescendo, and a blaze of fire streaked across the sky, descending into the depths of the horizon before crashing with a flash of blinding light. The portal closed like the end of a cartoon.

"Don't you realize humans were made in error? They were here first. We are bipedal fungus that flowered on the wrong world. That meteor wasn't supposed to crash on this planet, and now we owe an evolutionary debt. Talk about obsolete?"

It was apparent Graham would not return from this trip.

The speakers were shy of a few inches to Ezra's face, and he turned away to delay whatever horror was coming. Graham's free hand raised with a dagger chiseled from a glistening black rock.

"I'm going to need one more head for this, Ezra."

Graham's bat rested by the door. Ezra, without hesitation, grabbed it and started swinging. Graham's arm bent back with a loud crack. The dagger hurdled over the table, lost from sight, and the stereo dropped to the floor. Ezra launched his right foot into Graham's chest, catapulting him onto the table.

"You don't understand, do you? It is bigger than you or me. These sounds are older than the fucking ooze that dripped off that meteor," He struggled to regain his stance. "You saw it yourself! The behemoths must roam free!"

"Go fuck yourself," Ezra slammed the baseball bat into Graham's head, knocking his eye out of the socket. Projectiles of broken teeth flew from his bloody mouth, and he collapsed with a thud.

Ezra exited the front door and looked out past the railing that was now completely covered in green mold and massive mushroom caps. The darkness surrounding the porch was shrouded in mist, and he could hear howls shriek from its bowels.

A flying reptile screeched from the mist, and violent gusts flapped from its wings. Ezra swung the baseball bat in a panic, barrelling into its gullet. The winged thing flung back into the haze with a painful squawk.

He ducked down to remain stealthy as he descended the staircase. Clumps of large ferns and extinct palms now covered the foggy landscape along with the mold and fungus. The giant egg cocoon, now cracked open, dripping with a green mucous membrane. The thing hatched.

Ezra tripped over the fragments of broken shells and scattered to grab his bat, grabbing clumps of grass instead. Beside him laid Ranch's shredded overalls with his holstered pistol. Ezra never shot a gun but figured this would be a great learning experience.

He refused to look back, determined only to escape to his car. Get to the car and drive far away as fast as possible, Ezra thought. I'll call Graham in a few days to see if all this was some misunderstanding.

Great plan.

Ezra sprinted across the lawn but heard it trample behind him, gaining closer with each ferocious stomp. He turned past the garage, and luckily it was left open. He skidded into the entrance and reached to slam the door shut, but a gray, scaly three-fingered claw clunked down, slashing his forearm upon the garage door handle. Ezra stumbled back at the sight of this abomination.

Two gray heads snapped their drooling jaws on a long, serpentine neck. A long-tail whipped around its body as it slowly reeled toward Ezra. Blood channeled down Ezra's arm as he clutched the pistol, hoping to aim at one of their heads.

He cocked back the hammer and fired a shot at the beast. His wrists knocked back as the bullet exited the chamber, missing the creature. Another shot fired off, and the bullet penetrated the soft pale underbelly. An exit wound burst from its spiny back in a parade of black blood. He fired again and again and again like he was letting off fireworks. A bullet blasted one of the heads into a bloody stump on the neck. The creature dropped to the pavement, and the remaining head let out a pathetic whimper before Ezra blew it back to the Triassic period with his final bullet.

"Space does not matter, Ezra. *Only time!* We must devolve and return the stolen earth to the Behemoths," Graham, no longer human, but a mutated reptilian speaking with a forked tongue.

One glowing eye radiated in the night, and puss-filled sores and tumors covered his flesh. He raised his hands; one held the blaring portable stereo and the other the black dagger.

"What the fuck is on that tape?" Ezra shouted.

Graham did not answer with words but roared in the language of the behemoths.

Ezra ravaged through the junk in the garage, searching for anything to save his ass. He flipped over the broken recliners and lawnmowers that crowded any walking space. A busted wooden workbench huddled in the corner, and he ripped out the drawers only to find the jingle of nuts and bolts.

He inhaled the stench of stale gasoline and accepted death as his only exit until his weapon found him.

In the corner was a rusty shovel, and he leaped over heaps of junk to retrieve it and strangled the handle.

Ezra charged out of the garage, and with a swift thrust, the shovelhead slammed into Graham's chest. His broken sternum sprayed a downpour of black blood, and Graham fell to his knees. The stereo dropped to Graham's hands, and the tape deck popped out. Graham let out a low-pitched shrill from a mouth of jagged teeth as Ezra yanked the shovel from his chest. Ezra chopped the shovel over his head until the stereo and the cassette shattered into only fragments strewn across the ground.

Ezra stared at what was once his best friend, "Sorry, Graham."

Graham looked up to Ezra and smiled, "We did it."

The shovel head burrowed into Graham's neck and his head launched into the air. Graham's neck stump ejaculated blood in pumping streams laying horizontal on the ground. The head tumbled after splatting the ground, blinking a few more times before all brain function ceased.

FLAMES FLARED up from Graham's apartment, and the stars were no longer visible. The dawn peeked over the spired hillside reflecting off the morning dew. He reached for his phone, but who would he call? The only person that would believe him is now decapitated. *Survival of the fittest*, he thought. He remembered what Graham said about one more head as he raised the black dagger.

Sirens wailed in the distance but quickly drowned out by the thunder. The ground trembled like an impending stampede, and Ezra heard them sing. Blinding light flooded his vision from the fiery glare that streaked across the sky.

BORN UNDER THE MASTER'S SPELL

Out of the woods like a drunken idiot, bumbling some bullshit as I emerged between two towering tree trunks. Cheap beer lingered on my breath, and blood and ash covered my body. Something was funny, but I could not for the life of me remember why I was laughing.

Flames licked the horizon before burning out into billows of smoke that drifted behind the trembling trees. Their leafless limbs bristled into the evacuated heavens. Starless, inhabited only by the tyranny of the full moon. The painful cries slowly faded from the bowels of the woods as the gateway sealed shut.

Fuck 'em.

Fuck 'em all.

Fuck the wretched world I left behind.

I felt no remorse.

Strange spells do strange things.

Fog settled on a graveyard, stretching before me, quiet and dark. Dew dropped off blades of grass with each gust of cold, biting wind.

It was impossible to count all the unmarked graves. Names, birthdays, and heartfelt epitaphs don't mean shit once you're swallowed by the earth feeding the worms. I guess this cemetery wised up to that.

I killed time kicking rocks, breaking twigs, imagining them as brittle bones. The fresh mounds of dirt grew larger farther out in the field. Some were big enough to peek above the layer of fog, like miniature mountaintops. My eyelids were heavier than hammers in Mgo. I tried to sleep on a grave, but a putrid scent hit me. My nostrils flared enough to shove a dead Kennedy up them.

Probably a dead rat, I assumed. A giant one.

Black shapes scuttled beneath the fog. Clicking and clacking accompanied a wet smacking and sloshing. Dancing on a hunk of festering meat...

I restrained myself from taking another step.

"Who's there?" I asked.

The shadows stirred, and I could not make out a human form. They twisted and turned in lumps of darkness.

"I'll fucking kill you!" I shouted.

Silence fell, and I could only hear a squirming sound.

A cackle burst through the silence. A faceless audience laughed at me like I was some dumbfuck comedian.

"You think I'm kidding? I'm not afraid to bash your fucking brains in. Do you know who I am?"

They didn't; nobody did.

Black forms erupted from the fog, flapping their wings, swirling the fog into a pillar of mist. Cold gusts brushed against my cheeks as I lunged forward.

"Goddamned vultures!"

They flew off in the empty sky above.

My foot caught something. Face first, I smashed into the

ground, caught in its lifeless grasp. That squirming sound louder now.

Bits of brain matter, skull fragments, and blood stringing from the massive orifice left the head of the thing nothing more than a smashed watermelon with frizzy tufts of long black locks. The mandible mangled, and empty eye cavities sunk like rotting craters. And all the worms. The worms. Slipping and undulating through old holes and new. *All the squirming*.

And the stiff got his stinking fleshrot all over my Moon Tyrant shirt.

I'm no expert in forensics, and this was definitely not my first encounter with a corpse by a long shot, but judging by all the nightcrawlers, shredded flesh, and that *lovely* scent, this wasn't fresh meat. Must have tasted good to those birds, though, good enough to mutilate them into androgyny.

Corpses are never a good sign when you're alone in the dark. That's just instinct.

Some quack said the goal of all life is death. They were right, but it wasn't worth scratching my chin over. In fact, I was sick of all the assholes running their mouths about the human condition.

Fuck the human condition. Who cares? That's why I got into this type of astral travel, to find a realm more fitting to my oblique perspective.

I was too exhausted for that philosophical shit anyways. Even the most advanced sorcerer can be drained of vigor by performing such complex magick formulas.

At the edge of the cemetery, a gloomy town awaited. Only vague contours of the buildings were visible in the nightscape, and a fantastic castle rose behind the town's tiny skyline. Its looming tower was without any identifiable religious symbol and surrounded by hundreds of cones crowning into tall minarets that shimmered in the moonlight. Its arabesque architecture was otherworldly in its mass, much different than the rest of the town's drab design. The sight was hard to focus on as it appeared kinetic, shifting like a Mobius strip, slowly morphing into obscure shapes and angles.

Amber light twinkled in the tower, and shadows crawled before its glow. God damn, I'd love to burn that fucker down, but I needed food and some fucking sleep first. Then I could focus on invoking more majestic animosity.

II

THE SIGN at the entrance named the place Kgnott. A subtle phrase marked beneath the n namesake read: *the perversion of dreams*.

Whatever the fuck that meant. As I said before, *strange spells*...

A wake of black vultures perched on the sign, and I inquired about the town's inviting slogan. Judging by the silence, they did not embrace newcomers. The wake followed me, a feathered panopticon. Their naked bloodstained necks craned and twisted, observing my every stride upon entering. A vulture with a bulbous jaundiced eye yapped as I stepped on the main street. They took flight, and I swear I heard them laughing.

Kgnott? Like a knot? The correct pronunciation didn't quite click in my head, but I didn't plan on becoming a permanent resident.

The moon shined brighter than the flickering streetlights, but I made my way just fine in their dim flare. Abandoned storefronts lined the street with pitch-black interiors, and the copious shadows created the illusion that they had human-like faces. The windows like black eyes reflected what little light there was, and the doorways agape, ready to swallow any intrigued pedestrian.

The dilapidation resembled the eastern bloc and the desolation of Chernobyl. *BITE IT YOU SCUM* was scribbled on plywood nailed over the meat market, and it smelled worse than that carcass in the cemetery.

An out-of-service ATM flashed green lights against the gloom of a boarded-up bar with *DESTROY YOUR LIFE FOR SATAN* tagged across. Damn, I would've killed for a drink; it seemed like my kind of place too.

My footsteps crunched on broken glass in front of the electronics store. Old televisions arranged into a pyramid were displayed in the shattered window, scrambling with static and flipping through random channels; fuzzy screens, rapidly switching between images of hardcore porn and snuff films until stopping on a news station.

A warped transmission trilled the newscaster's voice like they were speaking through an industrial fan. They introduced a deformed weather girl, her eyes melting down the bridge of her nose, and the channel spazzed out. *"What? Don't trust your tired eyes? We are born under the Master's spell."* Her voice slowly dropped pitch, and she winked before the screen lost signal.

"Hey, pal," a scratchy voice echoed through the streets. "Yeah, you!" He walked, standing upright, down the side of a building, just strolling across the bricks like it was nothing. His shadow shrank close to the sidewalk. The streetlights cast a rich contrast to the face. Inverted black triangles ran from his eyes to his cheeks, and at a distance, he looked like a clown with white make-up. I didn't see a red nose, but that isn't what makes a clown *a clown*, is it?

"I was beginning to think this was a ghost town," I said.

"Far from it." His wry black-lipped frown bent up to his white cheek in a smile. "Come over here. I might have some things you'd be interested in."

He seemed harmless, nothing I couldn't strangle if it came right down to it. Skinny as a shank, he jittered as he reached into his worn-out leather jacket and pulled out a cigarette. The lighter shot a bright orange flame under his mop of long, greasy black hair.

"Check these out." He pulled out a collection of polaroids from inside the tattered lapels of the jacket. "What do you think?"

The white borders framed *something*—these *things* were fucking each other. Those oozing flesh cavities in an orgy of madness—words really can't explain how intriguing yet repulsive it was, even for a veteran of anti-cosmic mysticism like myself. The most filthy of processes...

There were people in there, too—I think. Dismembered and contorted in bestial poses, giant worms wearing human-faced masks screamed while other abominations copulated. The foulest interpretation of Picasso's *Guernica*. Of all my mind-fracturing trips after days spent devouring sheets of bad acid, I'd never seen anything so maddening. I had to swallow the bile from my empty stomach in a loud gulp, but I couldn't stop looking.

"You alright?" The smile flashed bleeding gingivitis.

I nodded.

The white space at the bottom of each polaroid had different names and dates: *Buer-Oystein 08/10/93... Apol-lyon-Per 04/08/91...Qayin-Bard 08/21/92...*

"Well, this is what you're looking for right? It's why you're here. I got 'em for the low." His greasepaint-crusted brow cocked up.

"How about a cigarette, first?"

He chuckled, then a cigarette pulled from the pack. "I know what you want."

"Yeah. What's that? A cheeseburger and a handjob?" I hit the cigarette and exhaled a cloud of smoke. From the leather jacket, he produced a little flask and shook it. Talk about hospitality. I took a big swig and snuck a couple more in while he searched through his jacket some more, tossing out various knick-knacks like broken glass and teeth on the sidewalk.

"Ah-ha! Here it is." A crumpled wad peeled into a rectangle in his hands, and he handed me the photocopied piece of paper. A list of illegible scribbles scrolled down the side with a smaller print at the bottom. I couldn't help but notice the blurry image behind the text. It was another one of those repulsive polaroids but blown up in size.

"What's this?" I asked.

"It's a show."

"What kind of show?"

"Like the one in those pictures, but the real thing. A bazaar of the most extreme melodies."

"I'm going to have to pass right now. I'm starving and need a place to crash."

"Don't be a pussy. I can tell by looking at you that you've dabbled in some horrible things, right? This is right up your alley. Everything you've been looking for. Don't you really want to say fuck the universe?"

He was right. And I'm proud of it. I'd do it again and again and again.

"Who you calling pussy?" The lapels of his jacket gripped in my hands, I pulled his pale face to mine. He grinned like a grimy gutter with the mouth of a great white shark and the breath of a dead dragon. "Ever heard of the Last Kommand at Mgo? The Gala of the Black Sails? Do you know who the fuck I am? I'm— "

"Easy partner." He cut me off and dusted off his lapels. "I got you, but I'm talkin' extreme." His arms spread as far as they could reach.

"Nothing I ain't done worse before..."

"Well, you *need* to go to this show. Some great headliners have traveled great lengths to play for us. It's like jacking off to the porno pages and then getting some real pussy. A lot better than the photos. This is the real thing. And it's going to be packed."

"Funny. I don't see anybody anywhere."

"Funny." He started to laugh and choked, taking a drag off his smoke.

Vultures circled above, and my gaze shifted towards their aerial acrobatics. Their circle spiraled in a hypnotizing display. I felt myself being lifted up into the canopy of darkness.

"Don't mind them." He patted me on the back. "I guess that poor bastard's carcass I left in the cemetery didn't fill 'em up. Ravenous, insatiable, cocksucker, mother...," His voice trailed into indiscernible mumblings.

"Speaking of," I said. "How about pointing me to the nearest drive-thru?" I perked up.

"Ah, hell. There will be plenty of beer at the show, enough vitamins and nutrients in a can to keep you alive for a couple more days." He slapped my back. "And don't forget all the groupies. You'll be knee-deep in pussy. That will be sure to keep your ass awake. You might find a place to crash too, even if it is *in* the ground."

"What was that?" *In the ground?*

"A place to sleep even if it is *on* the ground."

"Fuck it!" What did I have to lose? *Nothing.* "Show me the way." The words fell from my lips, conquered by the triumphant beating footsteps that came around the block. At first, I thought I was witnessing a parade. Other folks dressed just alike walked down the street, hundreds of them. Long black hair shrouded white and black faces, timeworn leather jackets, and black jeans tucked into stomping combat boots.

Their skinny arms supported a few wooden coffins. An odd time for a funeral procession, I thought. But then again, look around. Kngott wasn't exactly Willoughby.

"Let them show you the way, my friend."

"I wouldn't want to impose."

"Since when do you care about shit? When does anybody

actually care about *anything*? We are all born under the Master's spell." He hopped over a giant fissure covered in weeds. His limp body flung through the air like he had springs on his feet, and he dove headfirst into the procession, blending into the crowd like a vanishing act. I couldn't tell anybody apart.

The vultures perched upon the coffins, first pecking at them with hollow rappings. Their heads looked up and stared directly at me, calling me, all together voiceless, but as one. Yellow-eye kept a watchful eye.

III

THE PROCESSION MOVED DEEPER into an even worse area. The crumbling public housing stacked into clouds of thick pollution and swayed in the wind. We winded around the endless trash heaps spilling from the alleyways into the street and knocked a couple of aluminum trash cans over. An opossum rolled over into a lifeless catatonic state as it feasted on the rib cage of some unidentified mammal with brown fur.

"Must be nice," I said. "Goodnight, asshole."

Behind the barred windows, thousands of tiny eyes blinked and blinked and blinked from misshapen faces smashed up against the glass. Hot breath fogged up as they watched from their cramped space like it was a holiday parade.

Iron gates slammed open from the doorways. Grotesque inhabitants poured into the streets, crawling on all four of their lanky appendages.

"Freak! You fucking freaks!" The drooling toothless mouth shouted. A deformed claw plucked one of the pallbearers from the group, breaking open his neck like a beer tab and turning him up. It slurped his blood and guts right out, then discarded him. The leftover innards hit the pavement with a splat and oozed out of the deflated pile of flesh. "Not welcome! Not welcome!"

From banana peels to rotten eggs, plastic bottles to toothbrushes, they tossed whatever trash they could find on the sidewalk. Even a used condom hurtled through the air and slapped one of the outer members in the face.

Glass shattered, and a bottle of booze knocked a few unconscious. They were left behind in the shards and 100 proof, to be eaten alive by the vultures and other nocturnal scavengers.

One of the grotesques lifted a massive amplifier over their pinhead, and it crashed into the front of us. Guts smeared across the pavement like a boot had come down on us. No matter, a simple fix. The survivors of this assault replaced the obliterated with grace, merging into the vacancy, casually stepping over the splayed guts and entrails and severed limbs. They all looked identical to me, so I paid no mind; it was smooth as bowing the strings of a cello. The process came naturally to them; none of them even shuddered.

The street declined, and the pallbearers strained to hold up the heavy coffins. The procession never let on to their strain like some fucked up version of Sisyphus.

"How far until we get there?" I nudged the person in front of me.

He muttered something, but I couldn't hear over the sudden blast of machine gun fire and missiles whistling through the air. I ducked down waiting for an explosion to blow my ass to hell and back, but I only saw bright flashes from behind the blossoms of buildings. With each rumble, brick dust drizzled from windows, and the street lights flickered.

He kept frowning and turned back.

I was expecting a tank to bust through a wall or a plane to nose dive into a rooftop, but nothing. The closer to the bottom, the more the sounds of armageddon bled into one droning buzz like tortured hummingbirds. The voyeurs in the windows dematerialized, and the blinds dropped. Footsteps pattered like scurrying vermin; they had watched enough suffering and grown bored.

The vultures kept pecking at the coffins, letting out irritated squawks. Yellow-eye waddled across the coffin lid and stopped to look at me.

"What are you staring at?" I asked.

The vulture laughed, and the rest of them snickered behind.

"What is so funny?" I cried.

Yellow-eye crept to the edge of the coffin and thrust its hooked beak before my face, and opened its salivating jaws. I broke out in a cascade of sweat. Muscles twitched and tingled from my fingertips and to my trembling knees. My vision tunneled into a swirling portal, peering into the vast glory, yet equally terrifying—sublime!—experience.

A dying microcosm drooled from the open beak. The spirit of death oozed like some phantasmal pollution in a dripping black infinity. Droplets fell; countless corroded realities and spoiled worlds splattered within seconds on the cracked asphalt of the street.

Have you ever listened to such multitudes of suffering? It is a piece of forbidden music. Sublime, I tell you! Something that should never be experienced. But I did! And I craved more. I wasn't quite ready for the whole thing yet.

The beak snapped shut. And the black bird shuffled back to its former position, crouching over the pallbearers.

I thought about that opossum playing dead. The involuntary response when the nervous system is overstimulated, they go stiff and shit themselves like it's the real thing.

I dropped to my knees, knocking into the others, and the rest of the procession fell like they were hit by a firing squad. The coffins smacked the ground, and the wake of vultures took flight. The coffins lay still for a moment until the lids inched open. The hinges screeched as skeleton hands reached out. A mop of black hair protruded and slowly turned around. The neck creaked like a rusted, unoiled gear.

The corpses turned back and looked at me.

I saw myself beneath the coffin lids, many versions; all of

them rotted and putrid with decay, but then they started to move toward me.

I went stiff as a mannequin.

Play dead.

IV

I WOKE UP IN A DANK, unearthly place, a poorly built cellar of some sort. The ceiling rose into a web of rusty, dripping pipelines intersecting around an open skylight that spat out moonglow between its bars, and the crashing waves of an unseen ocean roared from beyond.

"Hey, pal." A familiar voice echoed. "Yeah, you!"

"Who is that? Show yourself," I shouted.

Stepping down from a dark corner with black locks draping over his pale face, he greeted me once again.

"I've been eating cobwebs since the spiders all died," he said, crunching his teeth. A hairy leg hung from his lip before slurping it into his cheek. "And when the storms come, you can catch a drink from the cracks."

My face frowned, much like his.

"What is it? Too good to be under the yoke? It is all you need. Weren't you looking for food, water, shelter? You need to get your nut? Feel free to go to a corner. They're pretty dark, and I'll turn around. Or if you want me to help, I'll—"

"I'll pass," I interrupted. "I must have miscalculated something. I can't figure out where I went wrong."

"No use trying. None of us asked to be here."

The skylight framed the tower extending into the sky like a crooked neck. Silhouettes danced behind the window in the shroud of amber glow.

"Them. Get me up there." I pointed to the tower. "This has to be some mistake. An error."

"Of course, it is all made in error. Is this not what you wanted? You seek the darkness, the corruption of silence, violence, destruction. All the chaos that comes with those strange spells, right?"

"Can you get me to that tower or not?" I waved my hands like a frantic child.

"I don't think you're asking the right questions."

"Goddamnit! Listen, creep. I'm not getting stuck down here with the likes of you."

"But it would be so easy." We locked eyes. "To give in. We are all born under the Master's spell."

"Fuck off. And fuck the Master."

"No need to be hostile. You are always free to go."

Baffled, I cocked my head, squinting my eyes.

"Which way is the exit? I'm going to burn this fucking place down. And you're going to be in it, and whoever is in that fucking tower."

"You don't want to leave just yet. It's time for the show, down the hall, the stage. They came all this way to play for us. The most extreme."

"Oh, shut the fuck up already. You want to see *extreme*, you cocksucker."

I grabbed him by his scrawny neck and squeezed his Adam's apple beneath my thumbs. His flesh was rubbery and elastic like a cheap Halloween mask. The skin oozed between my fingers, and I pulled tighter. I could see worms writhing underneath his skin. *I heard them.*

The surrounding walls shook into violent slams behind them; the muffled howls like raped angels came from within.

"What the fuck is that?"

"Don't... you... like... music?" He gurgled in my grip.

The wake of vultures circled the skylight, swooping across the moon as they dropped altitude. Yellow-eye dropped at the edge, grunting and waiting to feed. Salivating from the beak, it began to open its mouth.

Somehow he slipped between my fingers as if made of sand. He darted down the hall with his head in his hands. He turned his head like a screw, and backward, facing me, he mouthed the words, "this way." And then adjusted his head to the proper position.

And I followed, our footsteps reverberating in the seemingly endless hallway. The worms squirmed louder than ever.

A small stage waited at the end. A crowd faced the empty stage, and the man rushed through them. His hands threw the audience out of his way like weightless blow-up dolls.

At the front of this stage, his legs bent back, and his limp body flung up the stairs of the stage like a crash test dummy. Strands of black hair slipped underneath the black curtain, and he was gone.

"Wait!" I shouted.

The audience turned their heads to look at me, cracking their necks, each vertebrae splintering. Their black lips frowned upon white, absent faces, never blinking.

The curtain lifted, the stage lights clicked on and flooded the stage with a burning, fiery glow. The audience turned back to enjoy the set as they disintegrated to ash and drifted into nothingness.

I realized there was no exit, just a performance to enjoy.

The score to raping angels.

The soundtrack of suicide.

The ejaculation of ten thousand serpents.

Shambala burned down to a cinder and returned to the worms.

And it was glorious, a garden of unearthly delights.

You, too, will witness such boundless art.

We all will.

Listen for the music.

Wait for the worms or play dead.

We are all born under the Master's spell.

HIGHER FORMS OF
VOYEURISM

I

"**E**rn! Open Up!" Her fists banged against the door, rattling the pictures on the wall. One fell, face down, shattering the glass.

"Hold on, Mel. Give me a fucking second." I kicked the blanket off and hopped from the couch. My depressed contours rose from the cushions.

The television glowed, frozen on the blue screen, the lack of signal much like my memory: a lack thereof. Vague recollections of the previous night went well with my morning pick-me-up, a combination of coffee, warm beer, and whatever leftover food was sitting out overnight. I'm sure the night before wasn't anything different than my typical regiment, judging by the mounds of fast food bags and empty beer cans. Get hammered, eat shit, and watch videos until I blacked out.

Video.

Singular.

The stack of VHS tapes on the table was a decoy. An illusion of choice. I had one pick. It was always the same.

"Vile sexploitation under the guise of intellectualism."

"Drugged-out, fringe, and dangerous."

"Not a documentary but an exercise in hedonism, violence, and the dawning wave of UFO conspiracy propaganda."

"Pure Bullshit." *That was my favorite of the endless scathing reviews.* Most critics deemed it unwatchable, others even claimed it had *side effects*.

Pussies.

It doesn't sit well with you. I'll give 'em that.

The flick got pulled from its screening run. A tax write-off for the production company. No skin lost. They claimed the original negative had been destroyed in a fire and all advanced screening copies removed from circulation.

Except one.

And there it was, sticking out of the mouth of the VCR like a tab of bad acid on your tongue, waiting to kick in and fuck your entire life up. All you gotta do is press play.

"Histories of Mgo" was scribbled on the edge in bold black print.

A film I am responsible for.

A film that, in fact, did fuck up my entire life.

I shoveled through the trash, trying to make it to the door, dreading dealing with my annoying sister-in-law. I checked the peephole out of habit. Paranoia, really. The last string of visitors have been nosy journalists, an insurance investigator, and some dickhead cops trying to pry open whatever secrets remain in this apartment.

I undid the latch and cracked the door open, concealing my recent life of squalor and despicability.

"Yeah?" I asked.

"Fuck, you look like actual dogshit." She tilted her head a little, raising her eyebrows. "You doin' alright?"

I turned my head back to the interior of my apartment.

"Yeah, just been—" My tongue dragged. "Busy."

"Can't call me back?"

My ability to bullshit waned. She tapped her foot waiting for my response. She exhaled, flaring her nostrils. Her impatience was a trait shared with her late sister, Mara. They shared many gestures, ticks, physique, and even a birthday. Twins. I could barely tell them apart. Something I never shared with Mara. I always assured my wife that I found her the most attractive out of the duo.

Mel barged in.

"What the fuck, Ern? How do you live like this?"

She navigated through the shit, avoiding half-eaten chicken wings, crushed beer cans, and puddles of unidentifiable sludge with each step. *A fudgsicle and maybe a slushie.*

She saw the videos on the coffee table.

"Getting back into the swing of things?" She shuffled through the tapes, naming off some of the titles. "Any Given Cumday, Serial Cocksuckers 6…" She named off the rest of the titles. "Oh, who could forget this classic? The Seventh Seal."

I wasn't watching any of those. And if I did, they would quickly be ejected in favor of my magnum opus.

I unwrapped a leftover cheeseburger on the table and chowed down.

I don't remember hitting Buggy Burger drive-thru, but I'm glad I did.

A few cockroaches scattered from the table, vanishing into cracks and crevices. I washed it down with a gulp of warm backwash from one of the many wounded soldiers lying nearby.

All of her color faded to ash. Her beauty wilted like a dying orchid. My apartment, my appetite, my life had done a number on her.

"You gotta get out of this rut, man."

"A rut?" *Did she really call it that?* "I'm trying."

"You found any work yet?"

"Who's gonna hire me? I'm either the washed up porn director, the director of the most scorned documentary in the history of cinema." I counted the monikers on my fingers. "Or the husband of *the* Mara Bakus."

My late wife, shrouded in more controversy than the film itself. It's in my best interest to not get into any of the details. Not just legal shit, but for my own mental well-being.

I shook a couple cans, found the one with the most booze leftover, and drank what I could get.

"Fuck, Ern. Look at yourself." Mel got serious. "So, I'm going to take initiative and get your ass out of here. Tonight."

"No." I dismissed her.

"You don't even know what I'm talking about, Ern."

"Don't bother. I'm not doing shit. I'm not going anywhere. So, fuck off."

"You're such a prick, man." She sighed. "You owe me."

"For what?" I knew what. Mel had been generously paying my rent for the last few months. Not only that, she genuinely cared about me. She believed me when the rest of the world turned its fucking back.

She pursed her lips. She didn't have to explain.

"It's at The Kastle."

"The Kastle?"

"Yeah. So, try to look presentable. Shower, shave, and all that. Put some pants on."

"No. No. No." I raged. "I'm not going around some rich yuppie swinger club."

"Shit, man, don't act like you live on a plateau of exalted morals. You're a porn director."

"Was! I *was* a porn director. I'm a filmmaker."

"You *were* a filmmaker."

Bitch.

"Why do you need me to go?"

"Well, for starters; fresh air, man. And Mara would want you to live again. She'd hate to see you drowning in your own filth."

"You're trying to get me on some social fucking rebound so a bunch of assholes can feel sorry for me."

"Ern, Cam Kastle has a shit load of money. And a lot of that investment goes into *things.*"

What things? She didn't say. Shady shit, I'm sure.

"His influence runs deep in a lot of circles, one being movies. This might be a second chance. A comeback." She smiled, hopeful for a semi-positive response.

"Yeah, comeback. Tell that to Mara."

Stillness. A parasitic nothingness crawled between us like a leech, feeding on our collective pain, our sad thoughts, our grief.

"Ern," she spoke first. "She was my sister."

Mel picked up the picture that fell from the wall. A large crack ran through the glass, splitting down the image of Mara and I before those ancient ruins. The Kingdom of Mgo, forgotten from the primordial reflection. A place of worship… and sacrifice. It tingles your skin as soon as you walk through the rubble of what once was. The thorned golden pillars that knock Ishtar from the seven wonders list.

She wiped a stray tear from her cheek and placed the picture back on the wall.

"Why are you going? What's in it for you?" I asked.

"I need to get fucked."

"Good for you." I applauded her free spirit.

"Okay, I'll see you tonight. Do not bail. I promise it will be worth it."

"How do you know?"

"Trust me, Ern. Do it for Mara."

She left.

I watched her warped frame vanish from the boundaries of the peephole.

II

I CALLED A CAB. I wasn't driving, I was drinking instead. Cops are fucking pricks around here. I'm still technically a suspect, but whatever.

I hopped in the cab and we skirted off.

"Where ya headin', bro?" The cab driver didn't even look back. His eyes just examined from the rearview mirror.

"You know The Kastle?"

"Shit." He muttered under his breath.

The twinkling skyline of Basin shrunk, swallowed by the horizon. The road extended to where the streetlights were far and few, burning out like cigarette embers.

"A friend invited me." I stared out into the dark woods engulfing this lonely stretch of country road.

"If I would've known. I prolly woulda got another clown to cover this route." He glanced in the rearview again. His eyes rapidly shifted from the road to me, watchful and leery. "Heard some shit."

"Yeah?" I wasn't interested. There's a lot of tired, superstitious nonsense that I can't cradle after knowing what I know.

"That place out there. It's in a bad spot, my dude."

"It's just a club of rich bohemians playing new age intellectuals. Don't make it creepier than it already actually is."

"Yeah, maybe. But what I've heard still gives me the chills. Dude that works the midnights used to drop some weird motherfuckers off in that neighborhood. Said he'd pick them up at the city dump. They'd call from a payphone out that way. And they all looked funny."

"Funny?"

"Funny. Like *off*. Dressed in all black like a funeral and they had make-up on or something. Said it reminded him of a

.rubber mask. One of the creeps talked like it was from a voice box. Robotic. Staticky. High-pitched and shit. *Kastle—here—money—thank bud-dy."* The cab driver imitated the strange passenger's voice with an even stranger tone. A hollow voice, childlike, similar to a ventriloquist with a dummy. An awkward silence followed after he did the voice. "I mean, that's just how he explained it to me. I guess it probably didn't sound like that."

He turned the steering wheel, following the twisting curvature of the road.

"That ain't even the weirdest part. One time, one of 'em dropped something when they handed him the cash. The bastards never tip, but this time a black worm dropped out of their sleeve."

"A worm?"

"I guess. Or a maggot. I don't know. Something squirmy and gross." The cab driver mistook my questions for skepticism and grew irritated. "That's what my homie said. Don't know what else it could be. And before he could say 'get your nasty ass out of my cab' they had scurried off into one of the houses." There was another lengthy pause as we pulled up to the cul-de-sac. "At least, this is what my homie said."

"What happened to the worm?"

"What?" He asked, puzzled.

"Nothing."

The brakes squealed.

"Here we are, dude."

I reached in my wallet for cash.

"Yo, hold up." His eyes squinted in the rearview. "I thought you looked familiar. You're the porno guy. The one that made that movie everyone was protesting? Ah, fuck. Now, I can't remember the name."

"Nah. Wrong guy." I tossed the wad of bills at him and hopped out the cab. "Keep the change."

"No. It was you. Your girl, the one that's missing. Shit is fucked up. Straight up, bro. C'mon, you can tell me. You kill her? Or did she—"

I slammed the door shut before he could finish.

III

I EXPECTED SOMETHING BIGGER. I always thought The Kastle would be some *Eyes Wide Shut* shit, a big mansion with fucking pillars and a solid gold door knocker shaped like a baphomet. Instead I saw a row of identical two story houses. An archetype for suburbia.

The Kastle was illuminated by solar powered lamps that lined the lawn's stone path to the doorway. The porch light was green rather than yellow like the rest of the houses, likely a swinger identifier to welcome visitors to The Kastle's clandestine decadence.

I cocked a half-smile, not overly eager. My posture was erect to insinuate that I'm not repulsed by the dawning human interactions of discussing relevant social issues or the flavonoids in a glass of warm wine. My knock on the door was light and non-threatening. Every move, deliberate. If I've learned anything in the aftermath of all this, it's best to not provoke people. Nine times out of ten, they've already made up their mind about you.

It's all part of the show.

Faint phantoms danced behind the thin sheers hanging in the window. Loose and free, gliding across the floor.

Fuckin' weirdos.

A sheer pulled back and a strange expressionless face appeared, surrounded by a multitude of waving hands poking out of the dark.

What have I gotten myself into tonight? My stomach turned at the thought of the initial greeting. I needed something strong to make me normal.

To make me numb.

To make me dumb like the rest of 'em.

The drunker I am, the less likely I am to ask questions. Less likely to think. Less likely to give a shit.

The door knob slowly jarred and the door creaked open.

He was holding a glass of bourbon in one hand and had a dope pipe tucked in his floral shirt's pocket.

"You cool?"

I nodded.

He packed the pipe with a sparkling powder and chiefed on it, engulfing us in a cloud of smoke that smelled like bug spray. He motioned to me to hit it.

Was he hitting meth?

"Save some for later," I said.

He waved his hands to clear the remaining smog. "My bad, man." He brushed the strings of grey hairs out of his face and rewrapped his ponytail.

"Ern, right?" His teeth reached his ears.

"That'd be me."

"I'm Cameron. I see you brought some booze." He laughed and tossed a light jab at my bicep.

"Actually I did." I craned up my right hand that clutched a 12 pack of Shooster's Lite.

"Lite beer?" His face drooped, but then he chuckled. "I'm just kidding. Come on in."

The music was faint, but as we made our way deeper into the house it grew louder. The thumping bass trailed through the halls, overpowering the rest of the music. Some Euro-electronica shit.

We walked into the kitchen, and I snagged a beer and put the rest into the refrigerator.

"How's show biz going?" Cameron asked.

Was he being an asshole? I couldn't tell.

"I don't know if I'd call it that. I'm no Errol Morris."

"And modest, too?" He stared at me, a tear streaked down his face. "I admire that."

Was he about to cry?

I chugged my beer and crushed it in my hand. "Trash?"

"Yeah, sure. Allow me." He tossed the can on the patterned linoleum floor. The kitchen counters were covered in a thick layer of dust. There was no table, chairs, glasses, or dishes. No appliances plugged into the wall. Only a refrigerator, stocked with nothing but my lite beer.

I grabbed another one from the shelf.

"I'm terribly sorry about everything. Mel has become a dear friend over the past couple months. I've hoped that our relationship has helped her through everything. Your wife was a trailblazer. Both of you, Ern. And I hope that I can help you in some way too."

"Thanks. 'Preciate it. It is what it is, though. I'll bounce back. That's all any of us can do. Now where's the good bourbon hiding around here?"

He chuckled and ushered me through a long hallway. The walls were cluttered with framed photographs of a family. Cigarette burns and discoloration littered the photos like exposure to a concentration of high heat. A scene of kids splashing around in a tiny swimming pool shaped like a turtle turned into a warped imitation of an ideal summer. School portraits melted to deformed documentation. One picture was completely blacked out in the frame.

"These your kids?" I asked out of politeness. I could care less.

"Them? Nah," Cameron said, dismissive and apathetic.

I didn't know how to respond, so I didn't.

The hallways dimmed into blackness. "Sorry, the house is full of electrical issues," Cameron said. "Been a problem since I bought the property."

There was a glowing contour, like candlelight flickering behind a curtain at the end of the hallway. It opened and I saw only a silhouette of Cameron dematerialize in a swathe of colorful light.

"Just follow my voice, but be careful on the last step, there is a bit of a drop," he said.

A drop?

A plummet.

"My beer!"

The ground broke from beneath my feet. The free fall was easily over a minute long and my scream seemed to be sucked away by some soundless vacuum. I felt cold, dank air gush through my fingertips. Chilled tear drops ran up my face from the velocity of the drop. An unfamiliar smell surged through my nostrils and it almost felt like water, but I could breath.

"There we are," Cameron said. His hand reached to pull me forward.

The black floor met my feet and I was standing among a gathering in a large circular room. The decor, the design; ancient and futuristic at the same time. A soviet union inspired interior. I patted my body to make sure it was still all there. I turned back to an arch built from black stones, etched with glowing motifs across the surface.

"What the hell was that?" I asked.

"I told you that the last step was a drop." He reached out his other hand, holding my beer. "Here I saved this for you."

"Thanks." I popped the tab and took a drink.

The walls illuminated displays of odd metallurgy. Weapons, I assumed. Not swords or daggers, but like primitive firearms. Elongated barrells etched with rivulets into the irradiated chromium surface fluctuated a vast spectrum of neon.

"I love the decorations, Cameron."

"Thanks, Ernest." He winked at me. "C'mon, call me, Cam. We're cool, right?" His playful tone faded. "It took a long time for me to track these pieces down. Sacrifice. Suffering. Loss. You understand, Ern, I'm sure you do."

I slugged my brew and kept quiet.

"Anyways, sorry for killing the vibe for a minute. Enjoy yourself, make yourself at home, please. Indulge." Cam returned to cheery and annoying.

A small crowd danced about the room to the thump of electronic music. Individuals hovered from one cluster of conversation to the next, some of them as basic as pedestrians crossing the street. Some were butt-ass naked, sipping on a glass of red wine or munching at the appetizer table that was full of squirming black worms. Muffled moans and grunts came from behind a series of vaulted triangle doors.

A few individuals stuck out. Tall, standing still as mannequins, dressed in black robes and hoods that completely covered the face, missing eyes and mouths, like statues of shadows. I saw them breathing, their chests, inhaling and exhaling. That's the only reason I knew they had to be alive. The fabric between their legs was cut open to reveal the genitals. Dicks hung and unshaved vaginas peaked out from the openings. A table of nudists wearing bizarre masks that only imitated the human face snorted a pile of sparkly powder through a silver straw. After coming up from a heavy snort, they laughed as they played with one of the black robes' limp dick.

A hand waved from a stray group coming down a hallway and I heard my name. The voice wasn't hard to identify. "Yo Ern!" Mel ran up and hugged me. She was drenched in sweat and her hair frizzed out. Cam patted my back and said we would all chat later.

"You actually showed up? Wow, I'm impressed. Any trouble getting here?"

"Took a cab." I chugged some beer.

"You already drunk?"

"Nah."

"Whatever. I'm just glad you're out of that shithole."

"Cam seems cool."

"He really is! He's done incredible work with this place, huh?" She went on a brief tangent about his "work" that emptied my interest once she dropped terms like incorporeal transmutations or something like that. She continued pointing out various freethinkers and controversial figures among the gathering. Many seemed too doped up to even hold a conversation. "And then there's—You know, what does it matter who these people are. Let's talk first. Loosen up, man."

"Yeah, that fucking fall loosened me right up. I 'bout shit myself."

"Yeah, I can never get used to that."

"I know what this is."

"I hope you're not mad."

"No, c'mon, though. This is the same shit that got into Mara's head."

"Hold up!" She put her hands on my chest. Slightly slurring. "You made the movie, not me."

"I did. And I regret it. I regret ever listening to Mara's bullshit. I should've left her when she started going off about Mgo and the sex rituals. Because now, look at me."

Another beer down. Need another.

"Have some respect for your wife, Ern. Shame on you for even saying you regret it. Your film changed things. You showed others that Mgo was real. Mara saw it through the keyhole."

"Oh, fuck, Mel. Keyhole? They got you, too. Mara is

gone because of all this." I waved my arms around, trying to encompass the vicinity.

"Please, listen. Calm down. " She rubbed down my lower back. Her hand grazed my hip. She looked at me. "Let's go get a drink. Cameron will explain better than I can."

"He better have some strong shit."

VI

CAMERON WAS SLUMPED in a leather chair, not totally shot, but drunk enough to where his confidence rubbed off in his slacked body language. He slung a couple rocks glasses and filled 'em with some bourbon. He handed us our glasses and sipped his drink while he walked back to his chair. I swirled the liquid in my glass and sloppily knocked the whole thing back.

"We need you," Cameron said. He was dead serious. There was not a fragment of satire. His voice was cold.

Nothing was supposed to be funny.

"Me?" I couldn't help but laugh. Maybe, it was the heavy buzz from the booze.

"The Histories of Mgo. I owe everything to it."

I gleaned at Mel and she was staring back at me with that stone face. It was almost inhuman and it was the same face Mara had. "Yeah? Well, it took everything from me."

"I really am sorry about Mara."

"Of course, you are." I didn't have anything to talk about anymore. "Thanks for the top shelf, but I've got some shitty beers to finish."

I turned to exit.

"You saw them, Ern." Cameron said. "You found Mgo."

"Man, I didn't see them. I shut my eyes. It felt like fire, like staring at the sun. But Mara couldn't stop looking, I guess."

"Ern." Mel rubbed my lower back. Longer this time. Her finger ran up my spine.

"We were normal once. Enjoying a cyclical ignorant existence. Then she said she'd met some friends. Ones that had money for her experiments. Got into the dope and ritual shit. She even fucked different after that. And I followed her. I went along with it. I thought it meant something important on a spiritual level. I believed it." I sucked air between my teeth. Trying to get through it. "I still do, just not in that divine church type of way. My approach is I'm not fucking with it. I'll stick with watching the movie."

All I could do was drink about it.

"We are saddened about Mara's transmutations. But—."

"Again with that fucking word." They were unamused with my distasteful laughter. "Mara was charred. There were fucking worms eating her skeletal remains, feasting on black ash. Didn't see that shit in the flick. Did you? DID YOU?!" I slammed my glass down. "Had to cut that shit out for a rating. But don't worry, I'll let ya see a director's cut." I turned to leave.

"I have one." Cameron said.

Cameron flipped an unseen switch behind a cabinet and the wall adjacent to it rose up, revealing a large projector screen. The lights dimmed and the sound of the projector could be heard from behind as the beam emanated onto the screen.

The Histories of Mgo.
An Ernest Backus Film.
My stomach churned.
"The negative. How?"
Cameron grinned. I didn't need an answer.

"Ern, you did not give them what they wanted. They were unamused with your offering. They want violence and lust. For you to *feel*." Cameron fired up the bowl in his pocket and sucked in, his cheeks compressed and eyes bulging from the sockets. He exhaled the smell of burning chemicals. "Really fucking *feel*, man. I'm curious as to what they wanted with you two. I needed to find out, you know? I've dreamed of the dead emperors and their mutilated jesters weeping at the thrones. And when I saw your film, I had found the key to the gate. They brought us all together. To *feel*. To weep at their throne. Together. They crave it. It makes them cum."

He moved to a purple curtain behind his desk draped over a hidden structure and crooked his head around to speak.

"Ern, the thorned kingdom, the crawling shadows, the distant echo of their whispers. Mgo! You led me to the ruins, and I brought something back with me. This will be nothing new to you, but try to not look away this time." He drew back the curtains. Fragments of the onyx monolith stood before him. A clawed membraned wing of an unknown abomination was stretched over the gateway. The membrane filtered against an oscillating mass of bright flares of light.

I remembered the burning glare.

"Death's looming shadow," Mel said, softly. "They desire us. Can't you feel it?"

The torturous silence flooded with a clicking sound like a million crabs snapping their claws. The gnawing teeth of plague rats. Vibrations of decay and rot.

She unbuttoned her blouse to reveal her breasts and basked in its glow. Cameron followed by dropping his pants, his limp dick hanging between his legs.

"They don't speak. They just like to watch," Mel said.

Cameron shoved all the contents off his desk, the priceless bottle of Pale Bourbon shattering on the ground. He began to scratch away at the surface of his desk. Scrawls of a symbol developing under his clawing fingernails. Mel moved to me and began to kiss me. She whispered in my ear, "Mara wasn't ready. I am."

She climbed up on the desk and bent over.

"They are pleased. Can't you see them squirming? Go! Fuck her!" Cameron clutched the broken bottle with one hand and started yanking on his dick, trying to get it hard. He stabbed the membrane. It oozed black blood from the gaping laceration, exposing a flood of colorful light.

Mel arched her back.

At that moment. I looked. They saw me and I finally witnessed their glory.

Yes, what fucking glory!

I turned to Cameron.

"Ask them what they want." Cameron smirked.

Suddenly the light went into a deep purple, almost black. Starlight bled through the gate. They crawled closer, across a vast consuming negative plane, through all of our forgotten dreams of the thorned empire. Mgo. The golden phallus erupted from an exploding nebula.

I couldn't turn away. I understood.

My voice vanished in the vacuum.

They don't speak.

They only watch.

THE CHASM OF VYPRK

The chasm cracked. Odious fumes seeped between jagged and broken rock formations.

This was it! The entrance…

The twin suns drifted behind the rolling hills of Mgo into their nocturnal slumber. Bacchi considered returning to a nearby camp of nomadic drolls before complete nightfall. They had told him of the noises they heard coming from these rocks. From inside of them. Strange sounds. Vile exercises of the malign and baleful.

You're certain?! Or was it only night's mimicry of preying jackals? Do not mislead me, fool! Bacchi yanked the nomads ringmaster by his gold chains and threatened him with a clenched fist and without warning.

If he did not descend into the cavernous entrance, all of this—that he endured—would be worthless He slayed the Beast of Zeval, rid the Outskirts of ghouls, and stomped the skulls of the subterranean vampyric cults hiding beneath his great city of Mgo.

But this.

Nothing could match this terror... Actual evil... Pure evil... Waited for his arrival.

Yet, that evil was patient. No—evil is a term for our physical realm. Evil is just the beginning.

In Mgo, it is punishable by death to whisper his melodic incantations.

Bacchi cannot and will not retreat. Confrontation was imminent.

Out here, in the dark, there is no law.

"Vypryk! I am coming for your head!" Bacchi roared. It rumbled into the chasm, and a cloud of three-winged chiroptera erupted from within. Bacchi slashed his sword into the flapping vermin until they dissipated in the glowing twelve moons, now arching over the hills.

No more pondering. No more hesitation.

Bacchi glanced one last time at the surrounding nocternity. *The stars; they dance in the majesty of cosmic emptiness. Is there a world without such horrors?* He thought.

She screamed. It howled from the chasm's inner arteries to its hollow heart.

Is there a world without such horrors?

"No, " Bacchi said.

Bacchi gripped the hilt of his sword with mighty calloused hands. The beating of his heart was vigorous. His nostrils flared, inhaling the rich, sulfuric fumes. He accepted he had no choice. It was no longer just a quest or some arcane rite of passage to behead the menace of Mgo... *Again.*

No, this was personal. This was revenge. Failure is a fate worse than death.

He leaped into the chasm and vanished into the fumes. The passage seemed endless. It writhed like a serpent. Caverns opened and closed, leading Bacchi to wonder if this was not part of Vyprk's magick. Bacchi could lose his sanity in his state of savagery if he were to fall victim to Vyprk's mystic styles. Bacchi's feet slammed into loose gravel, and he rolled onto the ground. He rose and dusted himself from ashy debris.

The ceiling of the cave was dripping with stalactites, and the walls were crawling with bioluminescent insectoids that had spent their entire existence in darkness.

HAHAHAHA!

It came from deep inside, echoing throughout the cave systems. The maniacal laughter startled the creatures to scurry into the deep crevices of the cave walls.

It was pure darkness. Bacchi was blind.

."Bacchi! What lies ahead?" The sinister voice echoed and the words jumbled together. "Perhaps, I should start cutting off this bitch's head to attract the bugs. May they light your way?"

Bacchi removed his sword from its sheath. The blade hummed, and bursts of glowing green orbs surrounded the weapon. The blade absorbed the orbs and ignited like a torch of green fire. A path was revealed before his feet. Decayed corpses littered along the edges. Victims of the undead sorcerer's timeless wrath.

A skeleton donned with a shield and rusted armor laid still. Strings of white hair protruded from the skeleton's helmet. Bacchi inched past the corpse. The skeleton's jaw dropped and rolled down its lap, crumbling into dust. Bacchi startled, slashed his sword into the skeleton, smashing it into fragments.

"You're not frightened by our old friend, are you Bacchi?" Vyprk cackled.

"Frightened?" Bacchi was humored by this vapid assumption. "Certainly, you know I'm equipped with the Blade of Mgo? If I'm not mistaken, according to the testament of my father, this is the very blade he used to cut off your head last time down in this dank shithole. It is you that should be frightened, Vyprk."

"Bacchi. Your father could not even keep me in the grave. He still feeds the worms in his desecrated tomb. I always come back." Vyprk screeched. "Always!"

Disembodied voices haunted his thoughts.

You can't die!

He shrugged them away and continued the path.

It was not the time for distraction. Not the time for fear.

Time melted away in the chasm. Time was drunk and groveled on its belly.

Each turn seemed to circle back to where he started. The same pile of bones or was it another one of Vyprk's forgotten victims?

The skeleton assembled itself into a grotesque imitation of the human form. Stringy hairs and teeth ran up and down the moss and mold overgrown on the bones. A jaw bone connected to the shattered fragmented skull and recited an ineffable incantation before taunting Bacchi.

"Are you growing tired? Take a moment to rest. I saved you a seat. We seek him for wealth, knowledge, power! The spiritual extraction from this wretched existence you fight for! But this isn't why you're here, are you, Bacchi?"

"Where is she?"

The skeleton shrieked and lunged toward him. He slashed his sword through its middle. The fractured bones flew apart and vanished into the engulfing shadows.

Bacchi basked in the glow of his sword, contemplating his direction deeper in the chasm.

Bacchi! Please, he's going to—Oh no!

Her voice was drowned out by Vyprk's hideous laugh.

"Zelmoda!" Bacchi trudged through. Slicing away at

whatever was before him. He was guided by those voices. Those insufferable voices from somewhere else. The ones that plague him from distant worlds. *Bacchi, this is your only chance. We can feel the threads of space and time pull us apart. It hurts. You must right your failures. KILL HIM! KILL HIM! KILL HIM!*

His flaming blade burned away the spiderwebs, uncovering a doorway with an iron knocker. Ornate motifs twisted into sigils and transformed before his gaze.

"Help me, Bacchi!"

The door was the only barrier between her salvation. His salvation. His redemption.

Bacchi kicked and smashed the door into pieces. His thirst for blood, violence, and decapitation would be satiated.

The lair had a rotten stench. Bookshelves, full of blasphemous grimoires and evil tomes. Bacchi noticed an empty slot.

He knew what book Vyprk preferred.

The book of forbidden truth.

The book of forgotten inaudible atrocities.

Histories of Mgo.

A worktable set up with beakers and test tubes twisted and bubbled with bright colorful liquids. And beside these illicit experimentations, in the center, the book was propped and opened. Several candles, melted wax, with flames flickering in drafts of cold wind.

An altar was erected in the middle of the room, covered in strange alchemic symbols and dripped with blood. Above was a hole in the rocky ceiling that peered to the night sky's majesty. The twelve moons illuminated her naked flesh on the blood-stained altar.

Lifeless and cold.

A black dagger stuck from between her breast as blood coagulated around the wound.

He was too late.

Bacchi dropped his knees beside the stone altar and grabbed her pale hand.

"Zelmoda, forgive me. I failed. I do not deserve life." Bacchi bowed his head and dropped his sword. The green, glowing orbs surrounding the sword slowly faded out, rendering the weapon useless.

In the corner, where no light reached from the burning torches in the room, a shadow grew larger. Black tendrils flailed around, growing into an amorphous darkness. Laughter bellowed from the shadow.

"Bacchi, were you too late? Shame on you."

Vyprk's form began to take shape in tiny particles among the amorphous shadow until his body was whole. His long black hair blew back over his purple cloak, and he floated down from levitation. His stride was more akin to a slither rather than a walk.

"Vyprk!" Bacchi grabbed his sword and lunged toward the sorcerer. Bolts of dark energy shot from Vyprk's hands and engulfed Bacchi. His sword clanked on the stone ground as his body began to float. Bacchi moaned as the dark energy pulsed through his entire body as if raped by lightning.

"Bacchi? Did you even try to defeat me? Or are you just that weak?" Vyprk said. "Your savagery may save *your* ass, but not always the ones you love. You misunderstand the concept of true power! A warrior—" He stopped. His grin exposed a mouth of rotted and jagged teeth. "My words are useless for you. I'm not your father. Confess your failure to him when you meet him in the bowels of rot and shit! That goes for all of you Mgozk. Your great city will burn!"

Bacchi struggled to form words. He gasped and clawed at his face. Without the Blade of Mgo, Vyprk's spells were unstoppable. The disembodied voices crackled in and out, but this time they were screaming. Multitudes of screaming voices vibrated through his body, parallel to the dark energy. *It burns!* A sudden jolt of energy zapped deep into him. HELP US! Again. KILL US! Again. Each shock assembled a hazy vision of looming faceless forms. The shocking continued, and the faces began to gain more physical features; a nose and a mouth, and eventually the eye color and skin tone became apparent.

"Not much suffering left in you. Don't worry, her blood has provided plenty of life for the gateway. The portal is opening! The black sun!" Vyprk danced in a vibrant show of electricity.

A fiery blaze of purplish light ejected through the hole in the ceiling onto the body of Zelmoda. Her flesh was transparent. Her internal organs, nervous system, veins, and skeleton were visible. The white light crawled and writhed over her corpse, devouring her body. You could hear it suction the flesh and muscle as it tore from the body. It gurgled and slushed around with each gulp.

"Yes! It is working. Now the sword!" Vyprk reached for the Blade of Mgo, but in his attempt broke his concentration on Bacchi's dark energy restraint. Bacchi jumped like a saber tooth at the sword. Vyprk smacked on his back, and Bacchi retrieved the sword. It ignited with green fire and urged Vyprk to remain in his place.

"After him Moq-ra!" Vyprk shouted.

A reptilian creature hung by its talons from the ceiling. Its scales shifted colors like a chameleon against the walls. Membraned wings erupted from the beast, twice the size of Bacchi. It swooped down exposing the dagger-like talons aimed to slash Bacchi's stomach. Bacchi reared back his sword as the reptilian familiar screeched in midair, and he impaled it through the chest. Vyprk shuddered and lurched to the altar. Bacchi removed his sword as the creature moaned on the floor in a growing puddle of yellow ooze.

"Stop the madness, Vyprk," Bacchi said.

"Madness?" Vyprk chuckled. "Who is more mad: me, transmuting the nature of reality or you, the brute, who tried to save a dead woman?" His laughter, the cracking of bones. "You should have seen her willingly offer herself to such a noble cause. She wanted it. This was all part of the plan written so long ago. She figured it out and stopped fighting. Her blood spilled for more than you could ever conceive."

The monstrosity of purple light devoured Zelmonda's entire corpse.

Bacchi had failed.

The entire quest was worth nothing.

He contemplated turning his blade on himself, but he had too much pride.

He would kill Vyprk first.

Bacchi charged at Vyprk with the blade and chopped at his head. Vyprk ducked, and the blade penetrated the purple being. Its irradiated flesh tore open. Bacchi struggled to retract the blade from the gash. Black liquid pulsed from the wound and consumed the blade. The liquid moved like shadows and floated in the air creating a black vortex. Bacchi looked closer and saw *things*... things unknown to even Vyprk's spellbooks.

Not even *Histories of Mgo* mention.

The blackness swirled and formed into kaleidoscopic shapes. He saw himself: *birth/death*. He saw *others*... Other worlds... Other distant lands disintegrated like sand in an hourglass.

"Elasnk Ect Yg Vestill," Vyprk muttered. His eyes closed and he inhaled a deep breath. "*The black sun.*"

"Vyprk? What in the twelve moons is this?"

"The worst of all possible worlds. I'll see you in hell."

Vyprk dashed to the black vortex headfirst. His physical form, swallowed. Bacchi was confused. For the first time, he felt powerless. The purple being squirmed on the ground, dying. It howled between shallow breaths. Each one farther from the next.

Bacchi remembered his last night with Zelmoda. Gazing into the vista of Qaln's skeletal ruins, just outside of Mgo border. She accused Bacchi of his barbarism; insisted he was no different than what threatens him and their doomed city.

What choice do I have? He told her.

Bacchi disappeared into the blackness, too.

And those distant voices finally died.

IT WORKS EVERY TIME

The A/C was shit. Even with the windows rolled down, the muggy air had the suffocating texture of a wet plastic bag. It was a tight squeeze. The rusted '95 Chevy Blazer was plum full with music equipment and five sweaty dudes hungover as hell and without even a roach to smoke.

It was Nort, the drummer, he was driving; Riley, the vocalist (not singer) riding shotgun; Sawyer, the merch guy; in the back with Michael, the bassist, and me; I play guitar.

We barely had room for our balls to hang between our legs. A massive kick drum obstructed the back window's view in a nodulous mass of guitar cables, cymbal stands, amps, and my guitar case jutted from the calamity like a black glacial horn covered in now-forgotten hardcore band stickers.

Despite the less-than-desirable sleep situation and a hard luck brush with law, this was it.

Our dream.

The dream.

We were livin' it.

Barely out of high school and were tramping our way

across the midwest's seedy underground punk scenes. Cheap booze, fat blunts, and headbanging converged like a car crash. Well, except Michael. He was straight edge but that didn't stop him from getting pussy.

The Blazer didn't run on faith alone. Dreams were inert fumes in the gas tank. A gallon of ball sweat couldn't keep the engine running. If it did, we'd never have to stop for gas.

Luckily, we scored a basement show in St. Louis before hitting Kansas City and Des Moines. Sawyer had gotten a number from some weirdo the night before at the show in Knoxville, mentioning a squatter house outside of St. Louis that hosts basement shows. None of us remember much about the guy, come to think of it. Sawyer swore up and down the guy was wearing a Limp Wrist shirt but I would have noticed that. We didn't give a fuck, really, just needed a place to play and a place to crash.

At first, we thought the number was a bust.

We're sorry you've reached a number that has been disconnected. Please, check the number and dial again...

"Sawyer, either you wrote the number down wrong or that dude was full of shit." Nort slammed the payphone at the rest stop. "We got no weed, no booze, and now we're about to be broke if we can't make a couple dollars between here and KC. And I'm not fucking sleeping at a rest stop again."

"Should've slept on the hood of the Blazer with me, Nort." I smirked. "It was more comfortable than inside the car."

"No, dude. I swear. I wasn't even that fucked up last night," Sawyer said, pointing to the number jotted in chickscratch on the back of a crumbled up receipt from Del Taco. He recited the number while Nort dialed again for the fourth or fifth time.

Nort's thick eyebrows shot up like Groucho Marx.

"Is it ringing?" I asked.

Nort nodded and started to speak once someone answered and abruptly stopped. "Yeah, Denial. That's us." Nort continued to nod, puffing on his cigarette, the cherry almost burned down to the filter. "Uh-huh…Yep…Okay." Nort scribbled the address and hung up.

"We good?" Riley asked.

"Yeah, I guess," Nort said, his demeanor, slightly confused.

"What's wrong?" Michael asked.

"Nothing. Guess they were expecting us," Nort said.

"See!" Sawyer threw up his hands. "Told ya it would all work out. That guy was cool, he wouldn't steer us wrong. You gotta have some faith, my man. Don't let a little bit of bad luck ruin the whole tour."

"Shut up, Sawyer." Nort hopped in the Blazer and started it up. "C'mon, let's hit it."

We all got in the Blazer and spent the morning on the highway.

Not saying much.

II

THE GATEWAY ARCH was a distant silhouette curving over a shimmering skyline. We were Dorothy and her dopey friends staring at the Emerald City.

The address led us to the outskirts of the city. Puddles of heat danced across the cracked asphalt. Cars stopped moving, most of them propped on cinder blocks. On each street, we turned farther from downtown and deeper into adjacent neighborhoods. Structures crumbled into the derelict villas of vagrants. Blinking eyes peeked from behind boarded-up windows as we passed.

The toothless grinned; the limbless waved.

An elderly man in a wheelchair knocked back a beverage snug in a paper bag, his scrawny arm struggling to lift the drink to his dry lips. Faded advertisements for Colt 45 malt liquor peeled off brick walls, strobing neon signs hung in the windows of vacant bodegas, and the billboards loomed above the overpasses like ancient obelisks.

One billboard stuck out.

A man smiled down from atop his hightower.

A real celebrity.

You couldn't escape his gaze from anywhere in the city. He was everywhere, on the walls, in the windows, and watching from above. You could hear his voice. It proposed the fine argument for the power of Colt 45. To drink from his 40-ounce was to drink from lacerations on wounded angels. A glorious gift from a drunk god.

Billy Dee Williams said it, so cool and convincing.

It works every time.

The Blazer whined, choking on brake dust, and we had

arrived at the squatter house, bumping Krucifix Klan. The place was rugged terrain. Black trash bags were taped over busted windows and there was no indication that the home was even occupied. It, too, seemed abandoned along with the rest of the neighborhood. A For Sale sign was stuck in every scorched lawn except for the rundown pile of bricks before us. The block harbored a few beatdown cars, one with a dick drawn into the dust on the windshield and the street was silent except for the whooshing sound of vehicles speeding over the nearby overpass and the faint humid hum of power lines in the dead of summer.

"Is this it?" Nort asked, hanging his arm out the driver's side with a lit cigarette.

"It has to be," Michael said. He stretched his lanky arm from the backseat like a tentacle and tapped the GPS that confirmed that our location was indeed correct.

We exited the Blazer like circus clowns stuffed into one of those tiny cars.

"I don't think anybody is home," I said.

"Hurry up and knock on the door." Riley was anxiously pacing, holding the ass of his cut off jeans. "I gotta shit."

"Go shit behind there." I pointed to a graffitied embankment under the overpass.

"I can't," Riley said, he chewed the inside of his cheek when he was nervous.

"Why the hell not?" Nort asked, annoyed. "Last night you shit on the rumble strip like you were a fucking dog."

"Because." Riley hesitated to admit the source of his anxiety, pointing to the billboard above the overpass. "Lando Calrissian is just fucking staring at me."

Billy Dee was smiling, cheersing his Colt 45 in the aged advertisement. The corners folded down, barely clinging to the surface, blotted with several tiny rips and tears.

But his eyes were untouched, as brilliant as if the ad was printed yesterday.

And the eyes watched.

They spoke of legacy without saying a word.

It Works Every Time

None of us repeated it out loud. Our minds recited the phrase over and over like a spell cast by a cult of warlocks. It meant nothing at the time but when I recount that night, it is at that moment, I think, that we crossed over into a place not just beyond the city's limits but into a realm that we would never escape.

"Jesus fucking christ, dude." Nort stomped over to the embankment and squatted. "I'll shit with you if that gives you some confidence."

They both squatted in the cool shadows but before either could defecate on the hot concrete, the front door opened. Two birdish humanoids, differing in height, hair color, and clothes appeared from the doorway. Beakish noses protruded from their face, and they spoke English but with an accent and an unfamiliar draw that resembled squawking.

They came into focus as we all approached. They were certainly human. A greasy blonde mullet draped over the tall one's shoulders, and a bundle of feathers braided into the party side. Stick-and-poke designs were tattooed all over his exposed skin, the artistic quality, far from the work of a Tebori master. Cut-off shorts reach well above the knee, and it was surprising his dick didn't sneak beneath the fray.

The other, short and round, rocked a stained Anal Cunt shirt and a battle vest covered in patches. American Cheeseburger… Snakebite Satan… Gravy Gnosticism… There were more but I forgot.

"Y'all the band playin' tonight?" the short one asked.

"Yeah. We're Denial," Nort confirmed.

"Sick, come on in. We got some leftover pizza if y'all are hungry." A slice of pizza hung limp in his hand. He took a bite and churned it between his cheeks. "I'm Ben, and this towering motherfucker is Kleft." Kleft didn't say much, he had the presence of Lurch from the Addams Family. His eyes drifted in the sockets, fidgeting occasionally, like he was watching bubbles pop

We headed inside. The interior was average in size, built for a typical single family, but it had like fifteen people plopped on the floor, sitting crossed legged. 40-ounce bottles of Colt 45 intricately placed within their circle. The group stared at us with the same droopy, bloodshot eyes.

A record player in the corner blared a Caustic Christ 7-inch. The smell of reefer was a lovely greeting after getting our stash lifted by those State Boys on a stretch of highway in Tennessee.

The group passed around a strange apparatus, referred to as: "The Lung." A device crudely engineered from some pop bottles and ziplock bags. However the intricacies of its design were alien to our simple methods of rolling up a blunt.

"Interesting piece." Riley scratched his chin.

"Hit?" Kleft asked, sounding like a caveman.

Riley sucked in the entire contents of The Lung, and their faces lost all color following faint gasps. After Riley exhaled a mere puff from holding it in so long, he handed it back to Kleft.

"Damn." Kleft looked at the cashed bowl.

The record looped with a crackling hiss in the background.

"Who's next?" Nort asked, giddy with anticipation. He was hit the hardest by the search and seizure from Tennessee's finest. He had grown increasingly irritated and pessimistic without his fix. Kid couldn't go more than a few hours without a toke.

"Nobody, ya boy k'd it. " Ben responded like a death sentence. "And he's 'bout to be real fuckin' high."

Riley now had the presence of a blow-up doll. He mumbled something, only to be interpreted as indecipherable gibberish.

"Goddamnit." Nort hissed and stomped to the doorway. "I'm going to start unpacking the trunk." The door slammed behind him.

Michael followed. "Y'all gotta get him some bud, or it's gonna be a rough night."

"You think he's gonna be alright?" Sawyer said.

"Who? Nort or him?" I pointed to Riley slumped into the couch, the stale-cracker stench of old beer wafted as he sat down. The cushions were crusted with questionable stains that could be anything from pizza sauce to a vast array of bodily fluids.

"Sorry, dude." Riley laid his head back and closed his eyes.

"It's all good, man. I'm sure we can get some more dope." I turned to Kleft and Ben. "Right?"

"Oh, hell yeah." Ben grinned. "You know the other band playing tonight, don't ya? Hostile Witness? They always bring the best shit. Probably could score a sack off 'em, too."

"Heard the demo. That's it." I nodded.

We stepped into the kitchen, bullshitting briefly about the rumors that had been circulating on message boards about Hostile Witness. A reputation of felonious activity and eccentric behavior. Stories were passed from scene to scene about orgies, drunken brawls, and a legendary giant bong that stood over six feet high.

"Can I get one of those?" I asked Kleft as he rummaged through the fridge.

Kleft nodded and twisted the top off a 40 oz, handing over the cold glass bottle.

"I've never had Colt 45," Sawyer said.

"Oh shit, that's all we drink here. Be careful, though. Shit will do you in real quick," Ben said.

Sawyer and I chuckled.

But Kleft's eyes pooled into a black swell. Neither Ben, nor Kleft joined us in laughter.

"Cooool." I didn't know what else to say so I took a big swig. "Not bad." I lied.

"You'll get used to it. And you'll love it," Ben said.

Kleft's black-pitted eyes rolled around like the dumb mogwai from Gremlins.

And his lips moved. "It works every time."

III

As CARELESS as he was about hygiene, Nort's attentiveness to his drums was on the level of an engineer. His drum set appeared to be assembled from a junkyard. Black marks streaked across the skins, and multitudes of dings depressed the glossy surface. But the sound was unmatched. Each strike of the snare like a furious judge's gavel, and the toms thundered from celestial chariots.

"Dude." I growled. "Let me tune this shit real quick. It literally takes two fucking seconds."

Nort hit the snare again.

And again, slower and heavier, antagonizing my existence.

"C'mon!" I threw my hands to the ceiling, defeated. The guitar dangled across my chest. "I'm done." Both drumsticks smack the snare once more. He strolled around the drumset with a devious grin, posted up beside me, and reached out. "Here let me help you tune it." He twisted the knobs on my headstock and got my shit all out of tune.

"Seriously, man. The fuck?"

Nort moved to harass Michael while he was playing some licks on his bass. Nort did the same to him but much worse. Nort twisted the four knobs until it sounded like stroking an elephant's dick.

Despite their trivial qualms, Michael and Nort were a complimentary duo.

A hardcore Abbott & Costello.

They always seemed to get into little side adventures, too. The previous night, we didn't finish our set until after

1am. All the fast food joints had closed in the little town. The duo disappeared into the night and returned with a trash bag full of wings, ribs, cold beer, and warm pop. I asked where they got all this shit, and they said they stumbled upon a late-night barbecue a few blocks over. Nort smoked them out on a fat blunt and they passed out. Raiding the fridge for leftovers seemed like a fair trade.

"Sounds great, Fart!" Nort said.

"Man, Nort. I'm getting sick of you calling me Fart this entire fucking tour!"

"Chill out, Mikes. Don't blow your load before we even play the fucking show."

"Both of y'all chill." I snapped.

"Come on, Fart. Sounds like it's bumpin' upstairs," Nort said.

"God damn it." Michael shook his head, turning the knobs on his bass back to their proper positions. "All right."

There was a missing element to this conversation. Sawyer's commentary usually would tail end with some kind of positive suggestion of reconciliation.

"Where the fuck is Sawyer?" I asked. "He needs to get the shirts and CDs laid out for the merch table. We gotta at least make some gas money. I know we ain't getting paid for playing."

"Last time I saw him, he was yappin' upstairs," Michael reported.

The constant pop of snare drums and pulsing double bass seeped through the floorboard above us. Blast beats bursted in thirty second intervals, briefly pausing, then returning back to a sonic assault.

Probably Insect Warfare, I thought.

"Somebody's gotta have some dope up there. I'm fucking fiendin'," Nort said.

We entered the kitchen from the stairs to the basement. A smiling crowd gathered around the doorway.

"Fart!" It was like a surprise party. A roar of booze-breath laughter blew up the room.

Michael rolled his eyes. "Fucking hilarious, Nort."

"What?" Nort laughed. "Wasn't me!"

"Sawyer." Michael accused.

"Let's find the red-headed fuck," Nort said.

We journeyed through the sweaty skinheads, long hairs, short hairs, mullets, and chomo mustaches. It was sink-to-fridge with people, from old heads in Judge and Warzone shirts to Assuck and Leftover Crack shirts. They gathered in clusters on a black and white checkered floor. One kid was already passed out in the corner, taking a nap before the festivities began.

An earthen haze of pine and skunk permeated the air.

We levitated.

The curling fingers of the scent hooked our nostrils, drawing us closer, just like in the old cartoons. But there was no apple pie cooling on a window seal, only dope smoke. We passed Riley, still deflated on the couch, undisturbed.

Away we went, floating down the hall into a back bedroom.

A legion of smoked-out punks wrapped around a monolithic red bong. An idol worshiped like a stoner's up-in-smoke interpretation of Dagon. The red acrylic neck reached six feet and took two people to operate. A vortex of smoke swirled inside as the smoker lit their hit. Sure enough, Sawyer was standing on a chair, taking the giant rip. The water percolated and Ben slid the bowl from the downstem. Smoke emptied like an exhaust pipe and Sawyer collapsed on the bed in a coughing fit.

"Step right up! Hurry! Hurry," Ben shouted like it was a test-your-strength carnival game.

Nort's blue eyes shimmered in sapphiric flames. He was a puppy that found his momma's titty.

"Go! Go! Go!" The room cheered and cheered.

The bong bubbled like the experiments of an alchemist. Ben acted as the smoker's familiar, sliding the bowl once again for the next to inhale from the wizard's cauldron of black magick. Nort sucked down the hit and held it in with chipmunk cheeks. The blood vessels in his eyes, like crimson fireworks.

Applause became distant and absent. A faint whisper of smoke vanished from Nort's mouth.

Not a fucking cough was heard.

Nort lifted his hands like he'd vanquished a menacing beast in battle.

"He fuckin' k'd it," an excited voice cried before erupting in a rumble of cheers.

Nort crowd-surfed across the room, ascending from a surfeit of hands.

The hands...

Ben leaned the massive bong to Michael, but he politely gestured to decline.

I wouldn't say I exceeded my expectations, but I took an enormous hit. This bud was good shit. My lungs filled with nuclear ash, and my mouth emitted a voiceless scream... The language of fog... The cloud and fire from Exodus... Like I said, real, good shit.

I couldn't stop coughing until someone handed me a Colt 45. The generous hand was strange, disembodied with greenish skin, and cold fingers that grazed against mine. It was a hand with five fingers, yes, but it still appeared *inhuman.* An arm without body, a wilted sunflower in a field of wheat.

A voice whispered from somewhere unknown.

Yet, familiar.

It works every time

Am I this much of a lightweight? I thought. I was high as shit but reality had not completely dissolved. I had been half-shot for most of the tour, I needed to get a grip.

Some smiley dude with a bowl cut patted my back.

"What's… up… man?" I couldn't stop coughing.

"You're in the touring band tonight, right? Denial?"

"No… I mean… Yes… Guitar…" More coughing.

"Cool." He pushed his greasy black hair behind his ears. "I'm Kris."

I chugged the forty, followed by a loud belch.

"I feel fucking great." Riley showed up in the doorway, the aura of Spongebob Squarepants.

"This is Riley. Our singer," I said.

"Yo, I've got some merch out in the car if you want to trade before the show starts."

"For sure." I nodded. "We're actually looking for some pot. Anyway you could hook us up?"

"Yeah," Kris said. "No problem. No problem at all."

Riley and I left the smoke session. We passed Sawyer on the way out, schmoozing with a short, impish girl with a shaved head. Bad tattoos and sigils decorated her mayonnaise-colored skin; a face stamped on her neck below her jawline, unclear of who from the distance. Not exactly a 10, but hey, fuck it. Playgirl wasn't beating down our door to hang dong either.

Kris lit up a blunt and popped the trunk of his old beat-up sedan. He tossed us some shirts and CDs out of a pile.

"Thanks, man," Riley said.

"No problem," Kris said.

"Y'all going be playin' anything from that demo?" I asked.

"Nope. Just new stuff. Been working on this concept album for a long time." Kris said.

"Concept album?" Riley asked."Like the Alan Parson Project?" He joked.

"No." Kris said, sternly.

We were getting the vibe that this place wasn't much for joking around.

"Oh," Riley attempted to keep the conversation moving. "What's it about?"

"What?" Kris asked.

Nobody said anything amidst an awkward stoned silence.

"The concept album. What's it about? Like the concept?" Riley asked, again.

"You'll know when we play." Kris looked away.

Another rift of dead space between conversations.

Paranoia sunk in post-blunt. Kris's beady eyes darted around. He reached back into the trunk and pulled out a brown paper bag. He rocked it like a newborn with baby talk and giggling.

Goochie-goo. Goo-goo gah-gah.

When he started playing peekaboo it made it even more awkward.

"You guys want something to wash down this blunt?" Kris asked.

"Sure. What do ya got?" I asked.

The bag folded down to reveal a tall boy of Colt 45.

Why did I even ask? I thought.

"Gotta stay hydrated. We're about to play a fucking show, boys."

"What's up with y'all in Colt 45?" Riley asked, half-joking but with genuine curiosity.

"What do you mean?" His tone offended and his face went sour like he'd made out with a lemon.

"We just thought maybe you had some of the good stuff?" I played it off and nudged Riley."I mean, you got any Pale? Some good Kentucky bourbon, ya know?"

"Good stuff?" For a second, his skin looked like spoiled meat. "This is the good stuff. It works every time."

"Okay. Right. Ha. Ha." Riley dropped the inquiry. Kris was not amused in the slightest. "Give me the fucking Colt 45."

Kris handed him the beer from the paper bag. "Be easy with 'em. Be gentle."

We eased into our turn to head back inside. Then, I remembered to ask him about buying a sack of weed but saw that Kris was frozen. "You okay?" I asked.

Kris began to wave, but his arm was an unoiled hinge like the Tinman. Time faltered and ceased, his arm cocked at a 45-degree angle.

The front yard, the street, the neighborhood, like an abandoned film set; evacuated and artificial. The only animation was the city in the distance, blinking in a cascade of newborn dusk. The Gateway Arch bent, framing an exit.

I looked at the billboard. It was different now.

Billy Dee, now embraced by a woman. Half of her face was lifeless and sagging like she had suffered a stroke. Several hands reached from behind her; their flesh, tinged with green decay. I knew what the hands wanted.

Billy Dee still smiled. Only wider. His white teeth shining from beneath his mustache.

The slogan had been spray-painted, into a repeating ouroboros, around the edges of the billboard. The paint dripped into a multi-colored cardiovascular system down the surface.

...IT WORKS EVERY TIME IT WORKS EVERY TIME IT WORKS EVERY TIME IT WORKS EVERY...

IV

THE LIVING ROOM WAS EMPTY. Candles were lit and displayed throughout the house, flicking in the absence of artificial light. A terrible idea to leave all the candles burning but who was going to break up the party, the fucking fire mashall?

I blew out the candles.

"Make a wish." Riley joked.

"I *wish* we could find something besides Colt 45 to drink."

I took another swig.

The once-packed kitchen was abandoned like Chernobyl. I half-expected tumbleweed to roll by with whistling wind, but there were only crushed beer cans and cigarette butts. We finished off our brews and tossed them on the floor with the rest.

"Where the fuck is everybody?" Riley asked.

The door busted open.

Sawyer was panicked. "C'mon. I can't keep stalling these creatures. Y'all doing this shit or what?"

"Shit," Riley said.

The basement was at max capacity. Shoulder to shoulder. Negative space, nowhere between pounds of sweat-drenched flesh. Sawyer had the merch set up on the stairs. Denial Demo was written in black sharpie on the shiny CD-Rs and our shirts laid out on each step.

That girl was with him.

The one from earlier.

Sitting on his lap.

Her mouth opened to a tongue dripping with saliva. A bumpy, pink worm squirming and flicking his earlobe.

Sawyer didn't mind.

She cupped her hand around his ear and whispered something.

Her eyes shifted and focused on me.

I looked away, pretending to be examining our instruments.

There was no stage, just the floor. I'm surprised my headstock wasn't up somebody's ass.

I flipped on my amp. The tubes warmed up, faintly humming before wailing feedback.

Riley picked up the microphone and stared into the crowd.

"Yo!" His voice summoned silence. A majesty of mass control. A conjuring of crowd control. He paused briefly. "We're Denial!" He roared.

I slammed into an open chord and let it hold out.

Nort clicked his sticks.

1...2....3...

The audience went absolutely apeshit.

Bodies toppled over bodies to the riffage.

A mass of swirling chaos.

A guy with long black hair and a pot leaf tank top banged his head between the two voluptuous women on his lap. They jammed their tongues down each other's throats. The girls were conjoined at the hips, sharing a set of legs but two entirely separate upper halves. He pulled out one of their titties and started sucking until he faded between a colossal mass of flailing flesh.

The tempo drags in the final breakdown. I looked back at Nort. Life was draining out of him, but he somehow kept it smooth to create a triumphant conclusion to our set.

The audience applauded but was not satisfied.

They wanted more…

ONE MORE SONG!

Riley leaned over. "What do we do? We don't have any more songs."

ONE MORE SONG!

They continued.

ONE MORE SONG!

Michael and I locked eyes and nodded.

"Fuck it."

"Fuck it?" Riley asked. "What about Nort?"

We both looked back at Nort's posture slumped over his snare.

ONE MORE SONG!

The shouts transcended to indecipherable mutant shrieks. Words and language did not exist, just an unsatiated lust from another plane.

Nort wobbled on his throne. His bloodshot eyes fluttered and rolled. Did that monster hit do him in? Had Colt 45 made good on its promise?

Whatever it was, he was going down.

"Sawyer! Water!" I screamed.

Sawyer leaped over the drumset like a track star. He popped the top off Michael's gallon of water he kept by his bass rig.

Bubbles popped up from the opening as he chugged the entire gallon, overflow drenching his chin and cheeks. You'd have thought Nort just hopped out of the pool.

A jolt shot through Nort. Someone hit rewind, and he popped up.

The cymbals crashed.

I shredded a palm muted thrash riff, and as soon as it kicked in, like a catapult, a lanky dude shot over my amp, diving directly into the crowd and vanishing into a shrine of sweaty humans. Faces and limbs twisted and writhed like copulating serpents.

The song picked up speed. The hi-hat synced in. In the mass of undulating human body parts. Faces grimaced and frowned with anger invoked from the sounds we produced.

A fragment of time broke off, and everything slowed down into a blur.

There *he* was.

Billy Dee with a Colt 45, sweat dripping off the glass. He raised it high to me.

The image glitched as if it were some malfunction in his projection. Each time was like a stutter and his appearance drastically began to change. It was as if it were only a Billy Dee costume, or some kind of elaborate skin suit over something else entirely. The eye sockets sunk into cavities of emptiness. His cheeks sunk in like a corpse while he smiled. The drink slipped from his clutches and vanished before it hit the ground.

Someone must've hit fast-forward, Billy Dee dried up into a skeletal cadaver that looked like an ancient mummy. The skin was wrinkled up tight around the bones and started to crack. The limbs bent back, and continued to twist into an origami-like shape before folding into itself and disappearing.

The sounds of the mass mumbled gibberish or an ancient tongue unknown. A choir of drunkenness sang to them with devotion and clarity.

I knew what they were saying. I just *knew*.

It Works Every Time.

Time repaired itself instantly, as if it were just a millisecond of a forgotten day dream.

A brief hallucination? Surely, I'm past the boundaries of a light-weight, right?

A pussy. A bitch. A mark. A buster. Ho-ass boy…

Our set finished to glorious praise.

The crowd looked… normal?

Handshakes... Daps... Pounds came from all angles. Empty conversations about record collecting and past shows ensued and all seemed fitting.

Kris was by the stairs as we walked by.

"Fucking killer set guys!"

We all thanked him for his kind words.

"I don't know if we can follow your set, but wait until you hear what I was telling you about."

I couldn't tell if he was being a smart ass or what. I didn't care. I needed some water.

A hand popped out to toss a can of Colt 45.

Jesus fucking Christ...Fuck it.

Sawyer waved us over to the merch, and that girl was still there.

"Guys, this is Sasha."

We all greeted her with exhausted waves.

"You guys ruled." She grinned and licked her glossy lips."We should go upstairs and smoke somethin'?"

V

ATTENDANCE DISSIPATED. Great numbers migrated to places unknown. A wasteland of pizza boxes and Del Taco bags bled out with grease and an echelon of cockroaches. Beer cans, crushed. Bottles, drained. Cigarette ash dusted everything like the remains of Pompeii.

"Don't drink that!" Michael snatched a wounded soldier from Riley's hand.

"Why?" Riley, puzzled.

Michael examined the contents of the translucent bottle. He swirled around the floating cigarette butts inside the bottle.

"Thanks, Fart," Riley said.

"I should've let you drink that shit."

We sat on the couch and Sasha lit up a blunt.

I took a good look in wake of my fatigue and intoxication. I began to question my dedication to the lifestyle. I wondered if any of us planned to continue this nomadic way of life after the tour was over. Feelings like that happen when I'm fucked up. A shift in perspective, almost ashamed that I couldn't integrate into a normal occupation in society. Those emotions die quickly among the social distractions until things go quiet again, but I learned to bury the thoughts in a cloud of psychological oppression.

"Fuck, I need to take a shower." Sasha sniffed her armpits. Wisps of smoke drifted from her dry, cracked lips. Her plump thigh, a big sweaty turkey leg slung over Sawyer's lap.

"I haven't showered in…" I paused to pinpoint my memory. "Shit. Since we left Atlanta a few days ago."

"Two weeks for me." Nort raised his hand with pride.

"Goddamn, dude. You didn't even take one before we left for tour?" Michael asked.

"I forgot."

Shaming poor hygiene transcended to comical.

"It's been about three months for me," Sasha said with devout conviction.

Laughter died.

"Damn." Riley wrinkled his nose.

"It's all good." The joint came back in the rotation to her. "We'll all be *clean* tomorrow. You know what we should do?" She choked on the hit a bit and giggled. "Bathe together! Among the sewage and blood."

The joint made it to Sawyer, but we all paused and scanned the room before time kicked back into motion, perplexed by uncertainty and awkwardness, either from being stoned or the repulsive confessions.

"Yeahhhh." Riley was out. "I'm getting a beer. Anybody need one?"

Before we could answer, Sasha started kissing Sawyer. Her tongue danced in his throat. His hand popped up to pass the joint to Nort. Rotation made it back to me.

"I'm with Riley." Nort followed Riley.

"You hungry?" Riley asked.

"Always." Nort rubbed his belly like Buddha.

Sasha straddled Sawyer. Suckling noises at his neck, almost vampyric.

Sawyer's face emerged over her shoulder, shaking his head, and mouthed, *help.*

He fell back, eyes closed. Motionless; *something* put him to sleep.

Sasha's neck cracked, and her head twisted around like an owl. She crawled across the couch pillows, tossing them behind her as she made her way toward me. Her hand curled out like a tentacle, and she hissed with the breath of a rotting corpse. Her head bobbed above my crotch while she unzipped my pants. I felt slobber on my flaccid dork.

It wasn't right.

For most: a blowjob is a blowjob. Some horny fucks will take one from a vacuum, but not tonight. Not this way. I had a strong, intuitive thought that my dick was about to be serrated off. My brain felt scrambled up like an ancient Egyptian mummification ritual. A migraine from heck.

I started to follow Sawyer into slumber.

The front door swung open and smacked into the wall.

Kris and a guy in a Hawaiian shirt walked in. His shirt was open, and he held a box of strange devices with a unique metallurgy. A plutonium glow crept over his hairy beer belly.

"Woah!" They both shielded their eyes. "Starting early. I like," Kris said. They stared, waiting for the lustful procession to continue. They grew bored and continued into the basement. "We've got to set up. Have fun!" Kris's voice faded down the stairwell.

Sasha was disenchanted with our sleepiness and leaped over me to Michael.

Michael and Sasha went to town with each other, embraced by each appendage. Sasha appeared multi-limbed and slick with vaseline. "Fart, can you fuck me?" Sasha said.

Riley and Nort returned, cradling a few 40s. Frowns twisted with disgust as Sasha groped Michael's crotch. The outline of his pecker burst through his jeans.

"Yo, Fart, you want one? You might need it." Nort joked.

One of Sasha's arms unfolded from the human entanglement, swiped it, and popped the top. She chugged the whole damn bottle while thrusting the top deep into her mouth.

Our faces paled at such a sight.

"Damn, bitch. You thirsty?" Nort asked with all seriousness.

Her burp was drawn out and rumbled her bottom lip.

"We should go somewhere more private. Bring the gang, too."

Michael shrugged.

Riley violently shook his head. *No. No. No. Fuck, No.* If his body could speak. Nort, on the other hand, practiced a different kind of filth. He followed Sasha as she waddled out the front door, holding each of their hands, into the polluted night framed by the glowing arch in the distance.

Sawyer and I rose from the grave as reanimated corpses might.

"God damn. Something was off with that girl," I said.

"She was fucking nasty. I could smell her vag through her fucking crusty jeans. I mean, I don't smell any better, but holy fuck," Sawyer said.

"I thought it was my belly button," Riley said.

"I'm not talking about her fucking rancid stench. Her fucking energy or vibe or whatever the fuck. It felt like she was eating me." I confessed.

"You thought she was gonna bite your cock off? Oh shit." Riley was stunned.

"At first, maybe, then." It was difficult to admit without sounding completely stupid. "Put it this way, my brain was turning to cigarette ash."

Sawyer didn't say anything. Not awkwardly, but eerie. A clunking metallic sound came from the basement overpowering the strange silence.

"She was weird, for sure." Sawyer stopped. Terror embodied him. "I felt that, too. My head started to thump, so I laid back and fell asleep, I think. She whispered some awful shit to me."

"What?" I asked

"I can't remember, like a wall in my head."

"It was like 4 seconds ago."

"I don't know. She was just mumbling gibberish, right? Saying nasty shit in my ear like in some other language. But..." He tripped over a few syllables. "The words assembled backward or out of order, and it was a question."

"What question?"

"She asked if I believed in God."

"What did you say?" I asked.

"I said, yeah."

"Yeah?" Riley asked.

"Yeah. *Yeah.* So, what? We're not all cool atheists like you, Riley," Sawyer said.

"I just didn't take you for much of a believer," Riley said. "I assumed none of us were religious. The band name *is* Denial."

"It's not like a Christian thing. I'm not saying my prayers every night. I do believe in, like, a creator, deity, supreme being, *something.*" He declared his point.

"That's it?" I kept us on the subject matter. "Anything else?"

"Yeah. Then, she said, "I had no idea what it was like to be alone."

"The fuck does that mean?" Riley.

"Omnipresence?" Sawyer.

"Great lesson in faith, Sawyer. You learn that at vacation bible school?" Riley joked.

"Fuck off, Riley!" Sawyer screeched and withdrew. He looked troubled. His pupils swung back and forth like a pendulum.

"We should check on Mike and Nort," Sawyer said, against his usual positive outlook.

"Dude, they are probably just giving her the old in-out. I'm sure they will nut quick," Riley said.

" I need some fresh air, anyways. It stanks in here," I said.

The Blazer's cracked windows were pouring smoke like a fog machine. The old SUV rocked on the shocks, squeaking. You could hear the faint yelps of penetration.

"She's probably fakin' it. Those guys don't have that big of dicks." Riley said.

"Well, at least we know they're safe." Sawyer turned to me. "We were being paranoid. Thank God. Just some consensual safe sex."

"Yeah. I guess the dope here is just that good." Unsatisfied, I pondered on the cityscape before me. Grinding steel echoed and car exhaust tinged the air. Sawyer sat down on a lawn chair and picked up a big roach sitting on the railing. The end burned red and he puffed a couple times to get it going before passing it to Riley.

"Save some for the rest of us." Sawyer snapped.

Riley chiefed per usual and passed it to me.

I was hesitant, but the fellas stared back at me like I was nuts.

The Colt 45 billboard had changed again. I didn't mention it. I didn't need to add anymore to the paranoia in the atmosphere. I couldn't help but stare back at Billy Dee Williams. His eyes. Boils bundled on the sunken cheeks and the side of the mouth melted down. A large tear had been ripped where his nose was giving him the appearance of something almost-skull like. The woman was gone. He was alone. With a bottle of Colt 45.

It works every time. I mumbled the phrase under my breath.

"What?" Riley asked.

"Nothing."

The shrill of feedback emanated from inside followed by a rumble of bass and drums.

"Damn. Is Hostile Witness starting already?" Sawyer asked.

"I guess." Riley shrugged. "Should we go get Michael and Nort outta there?"

"Nah," I said. "When you need a nut, you need a nut."

VI

"PARTY REALLY CLEARED OUT," Sawyer investigated around the corners of the hallway. "I didn't see anybody leave or come back in."

"I don't know. Back door?" Riley carelessly strolled through the wrecked house, kicking bottles and cans out of the way. He yanked open the basement door and we walked down the stairs. The basement was completely empty. The floor, moist and damp. The air was thick with the musty rotten smell like there was something dead in a crawlspace.

"Where the fuck is our equipment?" I was pissed. Stomping through the puddles.

"'Where is everybody?' is the real question." Sawyer gently took steps, trying not to stray far from the stairwell. "Something don't feel right."

Near the farthest wall in the basement was a circle of empty Colt 45 forty ounce bottles propped up and in the middle was a little figurine. I bent down to examine it. It was an old Lando Calrissian figure.

"Are you fucking kidding me?" I asked.

"What is it?" Sawyer inquired. Riley and Sawyer leaned down beside me.

"Is that fucking Lando?" Riley laughed. "They really love that dude, huh?"

We looked up above the circle to a scrawl of graffiti that said that all too familiar phrase for the night. *It works every time.* Surrounded by strange sigils foreign to any occult text of our knowledge.

" What's with you people?" I shouted.

"What do you mean you people?" A calm voice came from the shadows hanging in the corners.

"Who said that?" Sawyer's legs were trembling. "Guys, c'mon let's go."

A small television flipped on from the other side of the basement. It wasn't plugged in, the cord was shredded like a rodent had chewed it up. It illuminated the dark, flickering between static and what looked like an old commercial for Colt 45. Billy Dee Williams was smiling. He was smiling at us.

"Fuck this." Sawyer darted to the stairwell. His feet thumped up each step. His right leg missed the last step and he flew backwards. His body bounced into knots. His arm whipped around his neck and his legs bent backward. He slammed on the dusty floor into a still torso wrapped in body parts.

We were too scared to run. We just stared at the screen.

Sawyer moaned. I didn't know if it was a good thing that he was alive or not. I was once again confronted with if *the dream* was really worth it.

"Are you thirsty?" His mustache moved above his lips when he spoke.

Riley and I looked at each other, waiting to see who would respond to an old tv screen first.

"No, we're good." I mumbled.

"Fuck off, Lando!" Riley yanked on my shirt to run, and darted toward the stairs. He barreled into a mutated form of Billy Dee. He went through him and out the other end. Billy Dee laughed and grabbed Riley by his shoulders. He lifted him overhead like a suplex.

"Fucking run!" Riley screamed, acknowledging his fate.

Billy Dee gripped Riley by clumps of his brown hair in one hand and by his ankles in the other, in a giant rip he pulled him apart like the flapper in a basket of hot wings. Intestines and entrails spewed out the bottom of his Meltdown shirt, from a fleshy fissure leaked black bile and blood. Billy Dee morphed his lips onto a proboscis, slurping the innards raining over his face from the corpse that has been split in two.

A scream was useless. I sprinted to the stairs, leaping over Sawyer, skipping every third or fourth step. "Have faith," Sawyer moaned, his limbs contorted and bent at acute angles. "I believe."

I had nothing to say. I left him there, my own friend, in cowardice.

I slammed through the basement door into the kitchen, landing face first on the linoleum and into a mass of empty Colt 45 bottles. I looked up from my fall and saw Kleft and Ben looking down at me.

"Hey bud, you need some help?" Ben reached his hand out.

Kleft was hitting a blunt and sipping on the bottom back-wash of a forty. He finished it off and tossed it beside me. The refrigerator opened on its own, the shelves filled with forties. Kleft grabbed one and started drinking another, never not looking at me.

Their eyes weren't looking at me. They were soulless vessels, under the will of another. I jumped up, retreating back from their reach.

"Back the fuck up." I grunted.

We danced in a circle around the kitchen in a bladeless knife fight. I was navigating my way into the hallway entrance for a clean getaway through the living room and out the front door. I prayed to fucking god that Michael and Nort were still in there fucking Sasha.

I prayed to whatever celestial authority would listen.

"Back up, motherfuckers," I screamed. "I mean it. I'm getting the fuck out of here."

"These things just happen," Ben said, casually. "Life on the road has its hiccups. You're either built for it or you're not, brother."

He was right. It was as simple as that, no explanation was necessary, nor was it wanted. Who cares? We're all going to die. Longevity and existential appreciation weren't our strong points and if they were, nobody had the opportunity to speak their peace.

"Fuck off," I said, gritting my teeth. I grabbed an empty Colt 45 bottle from the floor and tried to shatter it to use as some kind of weapon but the glass was strong. "Damn it."

I looked back to the basement door, I heard Sawyer crying, painfully. I refuse to repeat what I heard. His voice was sucked away by a loud vacuum. It rumbled from below, the entire house shook like an earthquake.

I started chucking the Colt 45 bottle at Ben with all the force I could muster. It made direct contact with his nose, pouring a waterfall of blood. Ben lunged at me, blind and enraged. He missed, hitting the wall. I kicked my foot towards his ass and he flew down the basement door, toppling down the stairs. He screamed, vanishing into the unseen abyss into silence, fading like someone was turning down the volume.

But I think he was happy.

Kleft did not move.

He stared at me, chugging his forty until it was empty.

The refrigerator opened again. Completely replenished and fully stocked, the light glowing brighter and brighter.

Kleft started on another one.

And I ran.

THE BLAZER WAS STILL under the radius of the streetlight. I yanked the passenger door and it flung open to a vomitous stench. Pussy, balls, and rot.

"Aye, what the hell?" Nort popped up from the backseat. "I don't know if there's anymore room back here."

Sasha's back was arched with her pimply ass raised high. Michael was railing into her from behind, and every smack of his thighs to her ass cheeks let out a whiff. Sasha moaned and her head cocked to me. Unnaturally, turning almost a complete 360. "The more the merrier," she squealed.

I was frantic. My words bounced between sentences in a jumbled mess.

"We…Got…Go…Fuck…Here…Now…Dead…"

"Dude, you are fucked up. Take it easy on the forties." Nort's dick plugged into Sasha's mouth.

I looked up at the billboard. Billy Dee was gone. A white empty space.

"Where is he?" *Did I say that out loud?*

"Who?" Nort asked. "Close the door, if you're gonna just stand there."

The door slammed on its own and the locks clicked.

A burst of muffle screams came from inside. Spurts of blood shot up on the windows and there was a screech from within.

A hand slapped on the back side door window, squeegeeing the blood in red streaks. A face popped up behind it. Sasha, but her lips had been peeled back over her face like a bloody mask. The muscles and tendons on her face, eaten with worms and maggots. The thing that was once

Sasha laughed through the window in a deep bellow and vanished back into the shadows of the car.

The moon swelled into a pregnant white bitch, swallowing up stars and space. All of St. Louis bathing in the moon's vomitous glow, a puke of white light turning everything just a shade paler. Its face, vaguely resembling a familiar face—*His* face— I don't even want to think about. It followed me and grew bigger and bigger as I ran down the street and it seemed I couldn't escape until I hid beneath the underpass.

But it was still out there.

Waiting for me to come out like an ant from an ant hill.

Watching me like a giant disembodied eye of a corpse.

I ran as far from the house as I possibly could get.

I could hear it behind me.

I didn't look back.

I had no intention to look back.

I never did.

VII

IT WAS dark when it most definitely should be the early hours of dusk. Yet, the sun's breaking rays were nonexistent.

The Colt 45 advertisements were all empty. Billy Dee was gone. For how long? I don't have an answer for that.

All the bottles in the images were drained and cans were crushed.

The party was over.

Blank slates with only the slogan, mocking me.

I made it to a corner street. One of the abandoned boarded up buildings we passed earlier. The old man in a wheelchair sat there, asleep. I panted beside him like a dog, resting my hand on the handle of his chair.

"Sir, please." I stopped talking and sat down on the curb. *What could this bum do to help me? Nothing.*

His crusty eyes opened and he rubbed them to bring his sight into focus.

"What's it to ya?" He lifted up a paper bag and took a swig. I didn't ask what he was drinking. I already knew.

"There's a house. Down that street. Just past the overpass. It's all fucked up."

"Mhmm." He took another drink. Empty. He lifted the drink above his head and tried to get the last drop on his tongue. "You got any change? A dollar? Anything?"

"No. Nothing." I patted my pockets.

"Well, what do you want then?" The old man grumbled.

"That house down there. People are dead. There's something there. It got my friends."

"All my friends are fucking dead," He took another swig from the empty bottle and handed me a drink.

I stared down the mouth of the bottle and it was full again. The old man nodded.

"Me too," I said.

And he said what they all said.

It Works Every Time.

"Every fucking time."

SUMMONING THE PALE ARISTOCRACY

A in't nobody cried at the funeral.

And it sure was a pretty ordeal.

The casket, a reflective black sparkling with shiny gold hardware, was kept closed, of course. Harlen *always* insisted his body be kept hidden during the service. He considered it a private matter. A delicate arrangement of honeysuckles and purple wildflowers drifted a scent down the aisle between the funeral home's faux-church pews that smelled just like Kentucky in the springtime. Folks dollied up to pay their respects, gently tapping the casket, silently gazing, then floating back to their seats.

Aside from the members of the Pale family, there were some mighty big names sitting in those rows. Some flew halfway across god's goddamn green earth to be in attendance to this service.

Abellone Vyssini, the Greek media mogul, sat in the front row with his new wife—or *girlfriend?*

Escort?

Whatever she was.

She didn't look a day over 17.

None of them ever did.

And he always had a new one at his side. At least, according to the tabloids Alvis saw in the checkout line at FairFood Groceries. That's just how the *pitas* out that way roll. *Polygonist?* or whatever they called that type of matrimony like them Mormons do.

Vyssini had a red beret slumped over the side of his bald head and his lady rested her head of blonde locks draping over his shoulder. Both of them with the darkest tinted sunglasses that must've cost a whole goddamn trailer park.

Alvis had met him once before many years ago at a Pale Company picnic. They were celebrating going public with their stocks or some kind of financial score. Alvis could give a shit about business. He was nothing shy of maybe 10 years old then and the memory was a fragment anymore, but Vyssini looked like he hadn't aged a day since. *A Mediterranean diet is s'pose to be plenty healthy. Must be all the kalamata olives and goat cheese.*

Most of the front row luminaries Alvis met at some time or another at one of the Pale picnics his Mom always forced him to tag along too. Across from the Vyssini's was Akeem Abadi, The crowned prince of *Kolambi* dressed in his thawb and aviator sunglasses like fucking African royalty should.

And just a couple pews back was the good ol' USA's fortunate son: Benjamin Colt. A buckwild oil tycoon with a penchant for poaching big game in exotic jungles and fast cars. His rowdy group of associates filled the seats dressed to the T with ten gallon hats, Ray-Ban Wayfarers, and snakeskin boots.

There was more, but Alvis didn't pay mind to those types of folks. *The filthy fucking rich.* So fucking rich they could wipe their ass with a few hundred dollar bills and flush them after shittin' in a golden porcelain bowl. Once you get that kind of wealth, your soul gets corroded to the point where it doesn't even count as a soul anymore.

The soul rots before the flesh dies and you're left with something primitive with a will only to consume and devour.

Humans can't handle power, they never have been able to. Alvis firmly believed that. And fuck, they were beyond powerful. These type of elites wine and dine with presidents, prime ministers, and dictators and convince them to keep the peace, invade, or pull the fuckin trigger on the big bombs.

The rest of the Pale family and friends took their seats in the back rows closer to the entrance for a quick getaway. They never got involved in all the high-society snobbery except maybe his cousin Karl. He was a real kiss ass.

The working-class Pale's were just happy that Harlen never sold out their jobs overseas to one of the commie bastards in Russia or China.

It ain't bourbon if it's made outside Kentucky state lines, it's just plain old whiskey.

While he was alive Harlen never showed much emotion, but he was proud of the Pale family and made sure they were taken care of.

Always.

Family was *everything*.

Mr. Frayser, Harlen's loyal assistant, approached the podium with a phantom-like stride. His thick Appalachian accent bounced and reverberated through the large chapel, making his voice sound as he were speaking with a multitude of tongues.

"Harlen was much more than my employer. He provided poor white trash from Carson County like me with an opportunity to see the entire world and meet many, many a-fine folks like yourself along the way." Vyssini and Akeem Abadi nodded. Colt whistled and tipped his 10-gallon hat off to Mr. Frayser.

Two rows of crooked yellow-stained teeth emerged from Frayser's lips.

He continued.

"I know Harlen would be pleased to know so many would come from so far to send him off to the other side. And it is great to see your faces in the same room with his kin. The great Pale family," his voice grew strong. "That helped build this dynasty from a few hillbilly moonshiners to the largest supplier of Kentucky bourbon in the world!"

The entire congregation roared with applause.

Frayser pulled out an antique decanter of brownish-red liquid and sat it on the edge of the podium. His arms bent up and his head craned down like an arachnid humanoid. "It's the real deal. We all know that. And it's damn good. The best." He eye-balled the bottle as he swirled around the liquor. The top popped and downed a long swig. His throat burned and he sighed.

"I always try to remember something Harlen used to tell me: *We're all related. We're all flesh and blood and bone. Swept up from the dust of this planet. That's family.* Then he'd look at me and ask, *"family is what, Mr. Frayser?"*

Mr. Frayser's eyes brimmed with tears, and one dripped down his cheek as he tried to continue on without balling. But he never cried. He sucked it up, snorted, and finished his eulogy. "Love. I would always answer: *family is love.*"

A collective silence filled the room and everybody seemed to breathe in sync. A consciousness under death's spell. The thoughts of the mourning congregation all joined like capillaries and arteries and veins moving through the body.

Rivers into a vast ocean.

An ocean of blood.

Alvis zoned out in the back row. Mr. Frayser's eulogy drifted into a faint audible mist. Alvis felt the foreign gaze from someone examine his presence. From his peripherals he saw the contours of a face. Vyssini's female escort drew her shades down the bridge of her nose and winked. Her grin lifted to her ears, showing a beautiful set of sparkling white teeth.

Their staring match was interrupted by the emergence of cheers and applause.

"Harlen, in the glory of death may you live again! Through us!" Frayser raised the decanter."To Harlen!"

"To Harlen!" The entire service shouted except Alvis.

II

It's been years since Alvis had gawked at the gothic pillars of the Pale Mansion, spiraling with vine-like motifs from top to bottom. The gaping mouthed gargoyle peered from above the arched doorway like a witch's familiar. Alvis pulled off his headphones connected to his Walkman. Buzzing guitars and the lycanthropic howl of Moonblood's song *Shadows* faded from the headphones to a faint buzz as the headphones hung around his neck.

Alvis wandered about the gigantic foyer listening to the muffled voice from the repast on the next floor up. A countertop poked out displaying bereavement cards and a leather bound guest book. As he signed, he noticed the rose gold head bust of what-had-to-be some *distant relative*. It glistened under the chandelier's light. A heavy brow and a Nietszche-stache hung over the mouth. The cold face glared with a vacancy.

He examined the bust in its familiarity, touching its nose and cheekbones. Thinking he may have seen it in a college art history class before he flunked out.

"Judging by your hands-on inspection, I take it you don't know who that is do you?"

Alvis turned to the feminine voice and said, "no, I guess, I don't."

It was Vyssini's girlfriend, she smiled and cut through him with her eyes. They were the color of glaciers and moonlight. "Well, you should. It's your kin. No offense, but that's kind of disrespectful given it's the old man's funeral."

"I'll be damned," Alvis said. It was his Papaw, all right. Art never truly replicates a face. There's always something off about the way the mind recognizes imitation. "Must have got rid of that stache at the turn of the century, huh?"

Silence. And a confused look on her.

Alvis fumbled his words. "So, how is it up there?" He looked toward the stairs.

"Just a bunch of old rich fuckers wolfin' bullshit."

"Why aren't you up there with them?"

"I'm rich by association, but certainly not old." She paused. "What are you listening to?" She put headphones to her ears. "Ugh." Her face soured like she licked a 9 volt battery. "Sounds like a bunch of bats. Who the fuck is that? Better yet. What the fuck is that?"

"Probably haven't heard of them." Alvis shrugged.

"You're probably right. Is that supposed to be scary?"

"I guess that's the gimmick they were going for. It sure as hell wasn't for the groupies." Alvis laughed.

"What's scary is you didn't even know your own papaw!" She pointed and gently poked his chest.

"Papaw? I know you ain't from Greece or wherever the fuck Vyssini is from."

"Because I'm from America. Duh. Born and raised right here in my ol' Kentucky home." She nudged him in the ribs with her elbow.

"How did you meet Vyssini?"

"Good story. I was sucking dick at truck stops just a couple months ago, then one of my girlfriends told me about these upscale orgies and well—let's just say I'm a happy bitch, now. If you'd like to hear the whole story. I'm sure he'd love to tell it. That is, if he hasn't already mentioned it up there in one of his circle jerks." She quoted with her fingers. "Want to grab a drink?"

"You old enough to drink?"

She laughed and turned toward the staircase, waving him to follow—no, *guiding.*

Alvis only came to sign the guestbook. *Really.* He

planned on going back home and getting plastered like he did every night on the free half-gallon provided by the Pale distillery. That wasn't pretty much the routine since college.

But, he could hear his mom's voice now…

Alvis Harlen Pale, you get your ass in there and pay your respects. It's your Papaw's funeral, for heaven's sake. You went to my funeral, now you need to go on to my daddy's. We all come from the same flesh and blood and bone. That's family. And family is what?

His mom's face materialized. Not as a spector. He saw the fragments of a smashed skull grow like rewinding a VHS. The red muscles formed from gushing blood spewing from the eye sockets and open jaw. Skin grew over the muscles like a festering mold. Black strings of hair shot from the follicles like spider webs. Eyeballs puffed up like small balloons in the sockets, and her tongue slurped in between the forming lips. Finally, she was a misshapen, grotesque head grown from the spectral emptiness.

It looked more alive than that bust could ever look.

She started to speak.

Straight to him.

FAMILY IS WHAT, HARLEN ALVIS PALE?!

His mother's voice trailed into a sequence of rhythmic echoes, each one dropping in pitch until they cluttered together into one droning gallop.

"Love." He said out loud. The hallucination ceased like it never happened..

"Do what now?" She giggled.

"Nothing," Alvis blurted. He squinted and pinched the bridge of his nose trying to think of what to say. "So, what's your name, again?"

"Betty Jo."

"I'm Alvis."

"Yes, I know," Betty Jo said, as if it were common knowledge. Alvis was the only heir to the Pale fortune. A fact who tossed from his thoughts like trash.

They ascended the staircase. Upon closer inspection, Alvis realized that this staircase resembled a double helix. The railing twisting seemingly at impossible angles into the air and arriving at a lofted ledge leading to the next floor.

"I don't remember much about this place. But I definitely don't remember this wild staircase."

"Been a long time since you've been here?"

"About 10 or 11 years. Around the time my mom—" He stopped.

"Died," she said. Alvis struck her with a glare. "I'm sorry. I just heard them talking."

"Oh, no. It's okay. I like to think suicide is a choice we have at all times. There's some nobility in it, I think. And not like cops or doctors gave any valuable insight to the incident, so I just assume the easiest and the least amount of questions. She was just ready to go."

An awkward silence assumed their conversation. Alvis juggled the thought of offing himself plenty of time, he just passed out stoned drunk before he could tie the knot. Loneliness could be drowned out by good booze. Pale was the best.

"It is quite a remarkable piece of architecture," Betty Jo said, shifting the conversation.

"Especially for being in the middle of bumfuck nowhere, Kentucky."

Laughing, they stepped from the staircase into a deep hallway decorated with an array of fine art. Oil paintings, charcoal sketches, woodblock prints, and even some abstract sculptures scattered down the way.

Strolling past them, they would stop and examine them to discuss them on a basic level of understanding. *This is cool.*

Wow, how did they do this? I love the colors. Alvis hadn't thought about art outside of his comic books since college. And even then, he was too hammered to care about technique.

"You like art?" Alvis asked.

"Not really." She pulled a vial from between her deep cleavage. Alvis tried not to stare, but she caught him and chuckled. "You want some?" She unscrewed the lid. The cap was a tiny spoon with a bop of white powder.

Alvis hadn't sniffed anything heavy since—again, since college. Hopefully it was coke. Whatever it was, he decided *what the hell?*

"Sure," he said.

A burn shot up his nostril to the back of his throat. It was like taking a cheap hook to the face.

"Holy shit!" . He wiped his nose. "That's some good blow."

"Blow mixed with some X. A little meth, possibly. Fellas we were partying with on the way here hooked me up. Best bang for your buck. I should've warned you." She sniffed her bump and turned to him and shook his shoulders. "Too late now! God damn, these are some really *really* great paintings."

"I thought you didn't like art?"

"I don't. But looks great right now. Real fucking cosmic. All the swirls and colors and shit. Feels like it could fucking swallow me up."

"I prefer sublime." He instantly regretted using that term.

"Oh, check out the big brain on Alvis. I'll take it, you like it."

"I find it interesting." He lied. "Took a couple classes in college." He lied again.

"Where did you go?"

"Miskatonic."

"I've heard of it. Some yuppie shit." She wiped the drip from her nose.

"Yeah, it was. That's why I flunked out. Or dropped out. Quit. Whatever you wanna believe." *Just be real, Alvis. You spent your time obsessing over your work, and not the curriculum. Had a nervous breakdown after you got the call your Mom was swinging from the ceiling fan in the living room. Haven't done anything but spent the last decade in a drunken stupor.*

"So, you work at your papaw's distillery now? A smart art-fuck like yourself."

"Yeah, free booze and good pay. I can spend my days off drunk and listening to bats."

"I'm surprised. You seem different from the rest of your family. Not in a bad way."

"I think that's why my papaw sent me to college and all that. He thought I wasn't cut out for labor intensive work. Mom said he always wanted a son too. Never happened. Lucky, my mom wasn't a lesbian or he'd be shit out of luck."

"Where's your old man?"

"Dead. I guess. One of those other situations I don't ask questions. Simple and sweet."

"Why weren't you close with your papaw? Seems like you guys would get along great considering the interest in the arts."

"He was busy. Traveling to remote islands off the coast of South America doing ayahuasca, spending time in Antarctica doing god knows what. Running a billion dollar Bourbon business was time consuming too.. All that wasn't my thing. I just wanted to draw."

"Apparently he did too." She pointed to a large oil painting framed in gold motifs of cherub-like angel-children. Indescribable at first glance, then shoved the psyche into a realm of unsettling aesthetics. The forms and contours brought to mind a specific painting in Alvis's mind he remembered from his Art History book.

Gericault's The Raft of Medusa.

Men and women, and small children on some kind of makeshift raft were being devoured alive, their faces shrieking as flesh tore in the jaws of a vile creature.

His mind wasn't putting things together. Something was off in his perception by the intensity of the chiaroscuro. He examined closer.

It clicked. It wasn't a beast eating these people.

It was all of the people twisted and contorted.

They were eating each other.

Phalluses penetrated orifices of such terrible sights in a gore-drenched self-devouring orgy.

All rendered in violent smudges and brutal strokes that seemed to be spattered in a reddish-brown ink. A scribbled signature was made out on the bottom right corner, but clearly legible with the name: *H.A. Pale.*

"That your Papaw's signature?" Betty Jo asked.

"Yep. Pretty sure."

"What's the A stand for?"

"Alvis."

"Wow, so y'all have the same name?"

Alvis nodded.

"Is this the kind of shit you draw? Big-tittied women and kids getting eaten by—" she had to find the right word, but couldn't quite bring herself to say it. "Monsters?"

"I stick to comic books."

"Anything I've heard of?" She lit up.

"No. I never made it that far and just gave up after my mom—" He rearranged his words. "After college, I mean."

"Maybe you can show me some of your old stuff sometimes. I mean, we both know people. Big people. You never know. I probably could help you out." She unbuttoned the top of her shirt slowly, exposing her deep cleavage. She gazed at him with her glacial eyes.

"But aren't you seeing Vyssini? Like… you know."

"Like fucking him? I mean yeah, but we're an open thing." She blushed. "Alvis,are you suggesting I want to fuck you?"

"Um, no. I just—" He began to tremble.

Music thumped from behind a tall pair of closed doors.

"Do you hear that?" Then, she flashed her pretty teeth. "I fucking love this song. Hurry, they are finally done with all the boring shit."

She yanked Alvis down the hall, almost thrusting his arm out of the shoulder socket. They rushed past other strange forms depicted among the walls. A sculpture sat against the wall resembling a debauched human form entangled in intestinal tracks like the tails of a rat king. Alvis didn't have time to ponder such grotesque thoughts. He didn't have time for anything. He was being dragged to a pair of tall wooden doors at the end of the hall.

The doors swung open into a massive crowd of yuppie fucks..

It was like a gallery opening. Art hung from panels cutting through the middle of the room. His grand-father's photograph propped up at the entrance was the only face he ever remembered. Stone-cold and no smile. Eyes empty. Glass eyes in a mounted deer.

The music stopped when they entered. The entire crowd froze up like someone snapped a polaroid. All with that same dead gaze in their eyes. *Emptiness. Soulless. Primal.* The brief second of silence was time being strangled and choked out.

"Alvis!" They all shouted.

The music kicked back on and the crowd smiled.

Handshakes and hugs came for him like spears and bayonets.

"How are you, sonny? You look just like your grandfather!" Colt swung his dick between his legs as he tipped his hat. *Why the fuck was he butt-naked?*

"Just like a Pale!" One of his associates shouted. He too was butt-naked except for a 10-gallon hat.

"Ready to take on the family business?" It was Akeem, smiling. Although he had replaced his Thawb with nude flesh.

The speaker system spat the plucking sounds of a guitar melody and bassy piano hits. The words trailed in from Three Dog Night's memorable hit and everybody started singing along.

> *Wash away my troubles, wash away my pain.*
> *I'm on the road to Shambala...*

ALVIS NOTICED several hands holding rocks glasses overflowing with the reddish brown liquid. A server holding a plate passed by with a tray of shot glasses. Alvis snatched one and tossed it down his throat. It burned like hot nickel and rubbing-alcohol. Nothing like a shot of the finest bourbon Kentucky has to offer.

There was no mourning. People were grinning like fucking clowns. Alvis noticed some of them actually had smeared red paint curving up their cheeks. *It's a fucking circus.*

He felt the booze hit him all too well. And mixed with that powdered potion he snorted with Betty Jo it got even stranger. What he witnessed was absolute hedonism.

Ecstasy.

Madness.

A party fit for Pan, Bacchus, and Dionysus all together.

The repast was an orgy. No wonder his family didn't come to this shit. They must've been turning a blind eye from this for decades. *Wait, is that cousin Karl?* Alvis thought.

Across the room, five or six women—they were so twisted up it was hard to tell which end was which—had spread out on furniture, getting thrusted into by other women with strap-on dildos. And sure enough, there he was. *Yep, that's Karl.* His eyes spun in different directions, gasping for air as he slammed his face into someone's asshole.

Alvis turned away. "What the fuck, Karl?" A lot has changed since the old days of renting horror flicks from Monster Video.

"Everything alright?" Betty Jo appeared like from a cloud of mist.

"No. I'm finding out my grand-father was some kind of sex-fiend." She nodded. "What is this shit?" Alvis demanded.

"Madness. Pure fucking Madness." A hand wrapped around her and pulled her close. "Oh, hey, baby! You know Alvis, don't you?"

Vyssini materialized with a crimson-smeared smile. "Not in a long time," he said with a thick greek accent. "I see you've met Miss Betty Jo. You all have a good time?" He raised his eyebrows. "Did I tell you how we met, Alvis?"

"Told ya," Betty Jo said before skipping off to a fuckfest by the sidelines.

Vyssini began to talk… Alvis wasn't listening.

Alvis scanned the debauchery. At a table by himself was

Mr. Frayser. Seated at the end, dining on a platter of rare meat.

"Will you excuse me for a minute, Mr. Vyssini?" Alvis pushed through the sweat and filth. Wiping his hands on his jeans. He dodged a wad of cum, shot from a cluster of flesh before finally making it to the table.

He scooted a seat out from the table towards Mr. Frayser.

The feast splayed out was something out of a fantasy novel, looking like shit Conan the Barbarian might enjoy dining on. Fresh grapes tangled on their vines ran across the ancient oak. Silver dishes filled with stinky cheese and bubbling dips crowded the center. But something wasn't right. The meat didn't appear to be like any livestock from the local farms. There were bones sticking out of a carved carcass. A ribcage hanging with crisp skin. He didn't want to say it out loud. He didn't have too.

"Say farewell to your Pappy, boy." Mr. Frayser wiped his mouth. "He was a true pioneer. Without his knowledge," he said and extended his hand. "His sacrifice. None of this wealth would be accrued. He brought this distillery from the old woods behind that dank shitty outhouse and brought it to the forefront of International Business. All it took was *magick*."

"Magic?" Alvis, puzzled, dared to ask more.

"With a K of course. Not some birthday party act. No rabbits, no white doves, no top hats. Only flesh and blood and bone."

"That's family." Alvis whispered. Without even thinking.

"That's right my boy." Mr. Frayser scooted his chair back, rose up, and put his arm around Alvis. "Come with me."

III

MR. FRAYSER POURED from the antique decanter from the eulogy. The reddish-brown liquid hit the brim of the shot glasses.

"This was the first batch your grandfather perfected. Saved for special occasions, I'm sure you can guess which ones count as special."

Mr. Frayser had an emptiness in his presence. A distinct aura of loneliness. Alvis had never seen him, not by his grandfather's side until today. He floated from behind the bar, passing a wall of ancient books. He sat in the leather chair across from Alvis. He grimaced after knocking back a shot straight from the bottle. The full shot for Alvis rested on the end table between them.

He waited to take it.

"Are you okay, Mr. Frayser?"

"I have to be, Harlen." He gulped after speaking his name. "I'm sorry, son. I meant to say Alvis. I'm a mess, you can tell." A tiny grin moved above his chin. He reached over and patted Alvis's leg.

"Please tell me that wasn't my grandfather's body in there. Please." Alvis started speaking erratically. "On the table. On the fucking table. Like a fucking Thanksgiving turkey half devoured. Because I don't think I can handle that shit right now." His mouth started running off again. "That girl. With Vyssini. She gave me some ecstasy or something and the liquor and the—"

Mr. Frayser held up his hand. Alvis stopped talking. As if by magic...*magick*.

"I'm going to tell you an interesting story. And show you some very

old things. You are free to choose to do with the informa-

tion as you please. I wouldn't be surprised if you ran screaming, but I suppose if you made it past the dining room then
you may be inclined to sit tight. Let me just say. Your
Papaw's Will requires this information disclosed with you.
This might save some time with all the lawyers and shit since
we're already here."

Alvis sunk into the black leather, squeaking as he sunk in.
He stared at the shot, but felt himself spinning and didn't
want to puke all over the nice egyptian rug in his dead grandfather's library. "Sure. Go for it. Let's fucking hear it."

"Very well." Mr. Frayser took another swig.

"You already know that your papaw came from a little
town known as Cinder, out in eastern kentucky. He was a
wild buck, I've heard. Of course, I didn't meet him until we
both enlisted when south seceded from the Union."

"Union? You mean the Civil War?"

"I see your time in Miskatonic must've paid off." He
joked. "We are very old, sonny. And we haven't always been
elite aristocrats either. We were gunslingers back then. He
saved my life, and we went a-wall. To think we could've died
for some insane construct like the American government and
their atrocities. We decided it was time to see the rest of the
world before it went to shit. Your Papaw knew that industrial-
ization and globalization would destroy earth's innate beauty.
The Panama Canal, deforestation, god damned automobiles,
nuclear bombs, and the list goes on and on of the terrible shit
humanity continues to do. So, we jumped ships and trains and
explored the world before it went to ruins. We stumbled on
something very old along the way."

"You expect me to believe my grandfather was over 100
years old? What did you guys find? The Fountain of Youth or
something." Alvis laughed.

"It might be easier to just show you." Mr. Frayser pulled

out a dusty spiral bound book from a shelf lined with various archaic texts *Rituals of the Black Sails, Histories of Mgo,* and *Cannibals and Kings.* "You know your old grandpa was quite the artist. And of course, this was before photographs had been as portable as they are today."

Alvis was speechless. He flipped through the booklet. He wanted to turn away. To shudder at such filthy things. But he couldn't. The vile sketches and sigils entranced him. The bottom of the page was scribbled with a now familiar signature. *H.A. Pale.*

"What is this?"

"Cannibalism. Isn't it obvious? It was the day we discovered the key to the gate."

"Are you saying that eating people makes you live forever? This is sick. You are all fucked in the head."

"It is the ritualization of devouring flesh!" Mr. Frayser slammed his fist and jumped up. His voice tinged with fading anger "The life force within blood and flesh and bone. Picking a vein from your teeth after eating a chicken wing is nothing like pulling tendons and juicy meat after eating the flesh of a femur.

"Your papaw met with sorcerers of a different kind. From a different world. Travelers. Just like we were. Exploring the bowels of what man could do. What man is capable of. Humankind's limitations. What he could eat. Magick must be performed with blood. Offered in flesh. And your talisman must be made of bone."

In the glass display at the book shelf, a giant bone was propped up inside under a beam of light.. Alvis assumed it was prehistoric, dating far beyond human record. A relic acquired by someone with tremendous wealth to showboat what they could buy. He couldn't be more wrong.

"This is the talisman of the first of our kind. Carved from

the bone of the abominations that walked before us. You hear tales of dinosaurs and mammoths. That's all ridiculous."

"But there is fossil evidence."

"Those fossils were incorrectly erected. Like a puzzle piece cut to fit the foolish narrative of the scientific institutions. No, what was once here were creatures that man should never lay their eyes upon. That's why *THEY* destroyed them."

"Who?"

"Some call them *AL*, others mention Cthulhu, Brahma, most cultures have a silly name for their creators and destroyers, but a real name cannot be pronounced in our tongues. If even attempted one might rapidly devolve to a cellular level."

"Right. Well, this is all nice, but I'm going to go back to the fuckfest and see if I can find some coffee and sober up so I can get the fuck out of here. Thanks."

"Alvis. You don't understand. The Will. Your grandfather is leaving all this to you."

"What?" Alvis turned back.

"Everything. The house, the business, the money, the entire dynasty."

"Why?" He fumbled his words."Why not you?"

"Although we are all *family*, as your papaw would suggest, I'm not of the Pale bloodline. As with the distilling process, the ingredients must be pure. And I still have work to do. I am your familiar, now. I follow your commands. Forever indebted to the family bloodline. Your mother didn't want to believe all this, she couldn't take the truth. She took one look at that sketch book and dropped dead. My gosh, Harlen was such a fucking mess. We had to do the whole suicide thing. It could've been her. But I promise you, I will never leave your side, son. You are the progeny Harlen always wished for."

"What do I have to do?" Alvis asked.

"Drink. Drink this. The blood of the ancient ones. The blood of our dead god. The riches are beyond this dying world."

Alvis debated on it all.

His troubles.

His pain.

His loneliness.

It was all over.

Alvis began to speak…

What would you do?

THE LAST KOMMAND

Commander Krazh was under strict orders to disarm and dismantle all weapon-wielding tribes. Most of the outlander tribes relinquished their weapons in a peaceful manner. The few that refused ended up—well, Krazh and his bloodthirsty battalion had a particular way of persuasion. Women and children were always the first up for collateral.

A few years ago, Krazh's leadership was already being heavily criticized for its barbarism, but it was officially subsidized by The Man. Back in the Kapital there was plenty of uproar from the regular activists to the comedians. On the eve of the Winter's Solstice, they flooded the streets and set all the trash piles on fire calling for "accountability." A couple State-boys got decapitated by Black Blades in the mix. Real determined individuals doused the heads in firewater and tossed 'em through The Man's residential quarter windows.

Kapital got bad off for a while, The Man shut-down the theaters(they censored all the good flicks anyways, by cutting all the good scenes out) and turned them into public execution stages. If you couldn't afford tickets, The Man provided all citizens with live broadcasts of the events on streetside projections. I actually got to see my favorite comedian make his last joke on my block, his battered face cast against the gray stones of my crumbling apartment complex.

The Fiends, as The Man referred to them now, snitched some names and still got thrown with the rest in The Kastle. From what I've heard about that place, it's fucked up. Apparently Krazh tortured a few of The Fiends for weeks with his unspeakable method of interrogation. One of them gave up where they obtained Black Blades, which are only intended for State-boys to use on criminals and undesirables. Outlander tribes had been supplying The Fiends with an arsenal of weapons wielded from black rocks that litter the outlands. The biggest monolith comes from Mgo.

I'm not mad. It is what it is, and I finally landed this job. I don't want to hear shit about morals, okay? I was sick of worrying about dysentery every time I scavenged for my dinner. Y'all that is judging me must be living in Topsa with the vapor pools and actual doctors, not the pill pushers we got in the metro. I heard Luxin has their own Shoka dispensaries. Must be nice. Yuppie fucks.

I am glad I wasn't drafted as one of Krazh's soldiers, though. I probably would have, if I had slept through Friday's Execution. There was a commercial for Krazh's campaign on one of the street screens. He was walking across a stage with our new crimson flag behind him, ranting about The Fiends and the Savages in the Outlands. "Among the starvation, the pain, the suffering. We are unified. Our dignity must be fought for with blood. The final enemy waits beyond our gates!" Krazh's mustache moved like a yellow-tinged caterpillar on his lips as he spoke.

I had no interest in joining, I'm a photographer not a soldier. I'd call myself an artist, but that would probably land me a few in The Kastle. But I'm assuming The Man wanted to prove that this campaign was following the principles of The Kovenant. At the end of the commercial a fast-speaking voice called for other jobs on the campaign including "Combat Photojournalist".

Like I said, I needed a job and before all this unrest there was no need for a photographer for any city publications when you're always on live feed.

I still had to follow Krazh's death squad across the continent and photograph some fucked up shit that

I'd rather not even mention, but we all gotta eat. At least, this was our last stop.

"REPORTER! WHERE IS THE REPORTER?" A deep voice rumbled in the mass of soldiers bringing their drunken banter to an inaudible silence.

Shirtless with an unloaded camera, I was already looking like a moron on my first day. Soldiers staggered to clear a path. I grabbed my camera, fumbling the roll of film before I could lock it in. The camera latched, and I slung the strap over my neck. I threw on a shirt too, but didn't bother to button it. At least I was prepared for my job.

A stout man holding a cigar stood at my tent. He leaned in closer and investigated the interior with swift glances. A thick cloud of smoke emerged from under his bushy mustache.

"Good morning, Commander Krazh. Doing well?" I asked.

"Listen, reporter. If it were up to me, I wouldn't have you follow my unit. Distracting us with pictures and shit could compromise our objective, but The Man insists all campaigns must have documentation,"he said with droplets of spit flecking my face.

"Yes." I wiped my cheek with the sleeve of my shirt. "That's what I'm here for, Commander. I promise I will stay out of the way. You can be certain of that."

"Certain? There is no certainty in war." He removed his cigar.

"Are we at war, sir? I thought it was just standard protocol for disarming."

"When you are with me, it is always war."

OUR TROUPE TRAMPLED across the plains toward a glowing citadel known as Mgo. The destination drew closer, and the sounds of clanking metal grew louder. Obscure figures emerged from the surrounding buildings noticing our arrival. Scarred faces of warriors observed the approaching cavalry while the women and children stood by their sides. They had not expected us. I snapped my first photograph. Inhabitants waved to our surprise. The Mgozk were known as superb warriors and master bladesmiths, far from a welcoming community. Krazh mentioned their rudimentary yet untamed customs.

"The Mgozk are primitive beasts. Unevolved! Lacking our intelligence," his fingers tapped his bald head. "They are only a few genes short of primordial ooze. I've witnessed them copulate with the wild beasts that roam the hillsides." He smirked, his mustache wiggling. "But they sure can make a superior weapon." His black blade slid from its sheath, shimmering in the sun's glare. A photograph of Krazh meeting the Mgozk leader, Zelmoda seemed appropriate. Probably make a nice cover to show the new "peaceful relations" we've achieved. She reached out to shake Krazh's hand, but he pulled away.

Snap.

"Damn it. Maybe, next time," I muttered.

Krazh frowned and mumbled something I could not decipher from my distance, but he pointed at a man hammering a strange black metal against a boulder. The man never broke his stride. The clanking echoed through the village. Melodic and rhythmic, like the inner workings of a clock. I headed straight to a busy marketplace. I heard Mgo has great Ale. Slabs of meat sizzled over open flames, and an abundance of colorful exotic fruit laid across the tables. A husky vendor shouted from behind a table of small black daggers. He grinned and pointed to my camera. A vast language barrier separated us, but I assumed he wanted a photograph. Mimicking snapping a picture with his hands, herepeated the word, "proof."

Snap.

The flash lit up his chunky tattooed face.

He handed me a black dagger from his collection.

"Are you sure?" I hesitated to take it.

He just smiled and waved.

The dagger was a masterpiece of weaponry. The handle was adorned in smooth ridges and decorative motifs, but the metallurgy of the blade itself was stunning. As with Krazh's black blade, it shimmered underneath the sun's rays. My fingers ran along the edge of the blade, and a droplet of blood followed.

Generous Mgozk approached with handfuls of fruit and legs of meat. Their fingers pointed to my camera insisting that I take their pictures. They all chatted in Mgozkian and in between bursts of indecipherable dialogue I heard the word, "proof" several times. I told them I would be back with more film. Grins flashed back at me as I cut down an alleyway.

Why would The Man be so untrusting to demand for their disarmament? Mgozk seemed peaceful—more peaceful than us. We were the ones that arrived with the fucking calvary in a trail of blood and tears.

The sun hovered high above Mgo, scorching the surface below its amber radiance. Sweat soaked my uniform while I strolled the dusty streets. At the corner, street clowns performed a comedic act for a small group of pedestrians. As the audience giggled at the cheap tricks of the clowns, I heard a whistle. A woman from behind a curtain gestured for me to walk her way. Tattoos spiraled on her body, growing from her arms to her neck and ceasing at the edges of her grinning cheeks.

"Hey, there soldier, care to share a drink with a Mgozk girl?" she asked.

I was surprised she spoke my language.

"Sure, I think I'm beginning to blister," I said.

"The Mgozk sun isn't too kind to Inland folk."

She pulled back a black curtain, and we entered a den faintly lit with the glow of several candles. A bar extended across the far side of the room, crowded with Mgozk patrons who nodded and waved. The girl walked behind the bar.

"All the ale you can drink," she said. A g'lac horn overflowing with frothy liquid slid over the bar.

"On one condition."

"Yeah, what's that?" I asked.

"Take my picture."

I laughed and took a big gulp of my drink. Are these

people that vain? Or have they never seen a camera? I thought.

"Sure thing. Can I ask you something?"

"Listen. You're cute, but this isn't a brothel," she said.

"No, I didn't mean that. What's with the camera obsession?"

"Oh, forgive me," She laughed from embarrassment. "But it is for proof."

"Proof?" I was confused. "That's what the folks in the market kept saying over and over."

Sudden laughter burst through the curtain. Footsteps patted behind the bar, and a boy jumped in her arms. She secured him on her hip and kissed him on the cheek.

"Aye, meet my savage spawn, Elos," she said.

I waved and smiled at the boy. I raised my camera, and the boy gasped and smiled. The flash lit up the den, and the boy dropped from his mother's hold and ran out of the curtain laughing. She waved and shouted something in their language.

"Elos. I've never heard that name before, and what is yours?" I asked.

"Elosinda."

"I'm surprised this place is so inviting to someone like me, especially given the circumstances for my presence."

"The Mgozk are used to this type of interference with our lives. If it's not our weapons, it's our food supply; if it's not our food supply, it's our Ale. Generations have endured this suffering for a long time, even before The Man." She paused with a strange gaze and snuck in a shot of some stronger stuff behind the bar. "Let's not spoil a good time with such drab discussions. Skul!"

"Skul?" I asked.

"Yes, skul. It means…" Elosinda searched for an adequate

translation. "Take. Consume. In abundance," She laughed. "Inland knows all about that." Her hand rested on mine.

I smiled. "Skul!"

The rest of the folks in the den shouted, "Skul!" Glasses raised to the heavens.

Laughter filled the room.

TOO MANY ALES stretched time thin. The sky was streaked with vibrant colors as the sun moved to the

other side of Mgo. The rhythmic clanking of the sword-smiths resonated as we drifted without direction.

"You can see the entire sky out here much clearer than it is Inland," I said.

"The synthetic lights of your cities obscure your vision. Here we can see the Black Sails patchwork as they guide us through the ever-expanding cosmos. Inland tries to make you forget what is beyond those gates."

"Have you visited Inland?"

"No, but Zelmoda has mentioned your cities, being the diplomat she is, we know of your Commander, as well. His arrival has been anticipated. And of course, Elos's father, he used to supply The Fiends with Black Blades for their liberation." She turned away, staring into the abyss above and changed the subject.

"Tonight is the Gala of Black Sails, you know? We've waited many, many cycles for them. You couldn't have picked a greater time to come to Mgo," she said.

Music overpowered the clanking metal and the crowded marketplace glowed with lamplight. Smoldering coals burned out to red embers in extinguished grill fires and the smell of charred meat lingered in my nostrils. Ale flowed like a busted hydrant into a clutter of g'lac horns from tapped barrels. Laughing, singing, and dancing feet shook the planet. Behind the score of their celebration, the rhythm was kept by the clanking metal sound of the blade smiths.. The invitation of Mgozk hospitality had enchanted me, but I had forgotten my job.

"Elosinda, I am sorry, but I must retreat. I don't think the troupe intends to stay much longer. They probably wouldn't be happy with my lengthy departure either."

"Yes, of course. I must be finding Elos before nightfall. Enjoy the rest of your time here. Mgo has many crooks to be explored."

I smiled and failed to think of anything to say except, "skul."

"That's right."

She vanished into a crowd watching the street clowns. The performance appeared to be a disappearing act of some sort. One of the clowns was shrouded in a black cloak making an odd buzzing sound. The other clowns snickered and moved under the cloak as if being engulfed. The shroud flew off and the clowns had disappeared. The crowd cheered, "Skul!" Then dispersed among the marketplace. My buzz was heavy, and I missed a chance for a great photo.

The fluctuating Mgozk melodies fell into its closing shrill, the voices of conversations went dead quiet. They stared at me making gestures like they were using a camera and clicking their lips mimicking the shutter.

The sound of clanking metal had suddenly stopped as I darted around a corner to get back to our camp.

KRAZH STOMPED THROUGH THE CAMP. Something must have pissed him off. He came barreling toward me through a mass of drinking soldiers. He made a signal to one and they began to unsheath their swords.

"Reporter!" he yelled.

"Yes, Commander Krazh?"

"Here's your chance to get some excellent shots. Just stay out of the fucking way. You don't want to lose your head."

"Why? What happened?" I asked.

Krazh shot a glare back at me that expelled the essence of destruction. The soldiers marched with their swords raised. Krazh rode his g'lac into the frontline and cut his black sword into the air.

"Men, we are at the final stop of our campaign. We have an objective. A duty. Each one of us plays a vital role in this campaign," he said. His sword swung, and he pointed it to me. "Yes, even you, reporter. Fuck peace. We're at war!"

The entrance into town was guarded by an entourage of warriors. Decorated flesh exposed ornate tattoos and deep scars of previous battle blemishes. They had been prepared for this day, as if they had already been aware. Zelmoda stood in front with a long sword crafted from the black metal.

"Mgo, this is my final demand. If you resist, you will be pulverized into an unrecognizable mound of flesh. Women, Children, all of you. Now, relieve your weapons, and you can go back to your diabolic ritual." Krazh shouted.

Zelmoda raised her black sword, "You have taken some of our culture's most precious resources time after time. But, to surrender our swords is to surrender our way of life, Krazh. Death before dishonor."

Krazh signaled the attack, and they charged at each other like crashing tidal waves. Headless bodies,

piles of intestines, and other body parts bestrewn the bloody battleground. I photographed Krazh skewer

three heads on his blade before kicking them off with his boot.

Civilian Mgozk ran for cover as the battle emptied into the marketplace. Hours ago, this was a

celebration, and in minutes it had become a warzone. Soldiers set fire to houses and buildings. It did not

take long for half the citadel to become a raging inferno.

"If you are not dead. Drop your weapons and run. It is over," Krazh shouted.

I lost count of the dead. Hundreds of casualties, I assumed. The photographs would provide more

accurate numbers. The soldiers entered homes murdering women and children. Infant cries fell on deaf

ears and their pleading mothers screamed in terror.

I refused to be a part of evil incarnate.

I couldn't stop thinking of Elosinda and her son.

I wanted to save them.

It was my only path to redemption.

ELOS WAS CROUCHING under a torn awning on the backside of the citadel. Just past the corner of the

market. He heard my footsteps and looked up with soot-covered cheeks streaking with tears.

"Go away! Away!" He screamed.

"Elos, please. Where is your mother?"

"It is too late." He bowed his head.

"Too late?" I feared the worst.

"Yes, too late for you."

The boy launched toward me. Fueled by vengeance, gripping a black dagger, similar to the one given to me by the vendor earlier today and… Forgive me. It was instinct. Fight or flight. My dagger submerged into the boy's chest and he gulped a few shallow breaths before his body went limp onto my shoulder. I slipped him off the penetrated weapon. I sat for a moment with my hands saturated in blood.

I couldn't carry the boy through the streets, so I wandered aimlessly among the destruction.

I held back tears in fear of Krazh's response to what I had done.

I heard his voice repeating in my head.

Fuck peace. We're at war!

War triumphed and I was dripping gore. I staggered near the marketplace and passed Elosinda's tavern. Breaking glass followed by a loud shriek came from inside. I ran inside. The bar was littered withcorpses. The smell of blood and ale tinged the air.

A group of soldiers had Elosinda pinned down on the bar. Her clothes shredded and nearly stripped naked. Cries for mercy did not affect the heartless and that is just how Krazh had trained them.

Fuck Peace.

We're at War.

I crawled in the shadows and ascended a banister that ran across the car. I gripped the banister and swung down like a dead man at the gallows. My body slammed on the back of the biggest one on top of Elosinda. My dagger wrapped around his neck, shredding flesh into a geyser of blood.

Another soldier chopped his sword, but my blade shot up and the handle laid flush with his chin. The force lifted him off his feet before he slumped into the floor. The last two lunged at me together. I sliced from his groin to his neck like unzipping a skin suit.

A pair of arms came from behind and restrained me. His strong grip almost removed the black dagger, but Elosinda kicked him between his legs, and he fell to his knees. My dagger penetrated the back of his skull. He let out a couple of squirms before going still in a pool of his blood.

"I thought you were—"

"I would be, but some things are willed only by the Black Sails," she interrupted.

I ripped down the black curtain at the entrance and threw it over her naked body.

"Elos. He is wandering the streets in this bloodbath," she said.

I didn't respond. I couldn't. Guilt and shame prevented me from exposing my murderous secret. She might have tried to kill me, and I deserved it, at least I thought so. I was as guilty as Krazh now.

We trudged through the now-dilapidated citadel of Mgo. Cinder and black ash made graves for the scattered dead. Elos's body lay face down. Right where I left him. She collapsed over his body.

Speechless; she could only cry.

I stood by speechless, but without tears.

"THE SAVAGES COULDN'T EVEN COVER YOU UP, my son." Her bellows were drowned out by the approach of marching footsteps down the streets.

Krazh and his soldiers spotted us. He grinned and lifted

the head of Zelmoda. Her mouth agape and blood trickling from her mouth and eyes.

"Ah, reporter. Today will make for illustrious documentation of our conquest. I can see it on the front page. Hell, you may even win some awards. Let me help you with a title for this one: A whore and her progeny," Krazh said. He tossed his head back and laughed. "Now go on take a picture before I kill this bitch. Or perhaps, you would like to move up in rank and do the honors with the black blade?"

Elosinda shuddered over her lifeless son.

"First you kill the boy's father! And now you kill my son." She started chanting a prayer of some kind.

"If I could take credit for the boy too, I would. Believe me he's not the first Mgo kid I killed tonight."

She continued to pray.

"Who are you praying to, whore? Your gods are not listening, or perhaps you are not loud enough?"

Krazh raised his blade to her neck and lifted her chin to his view.

Tears still ran down Elosinda's cheeks, but she began to laugh. Krazh pulled his sword back and sheathed it. His hands drew back and swung at Elosinda's face. She fell on Elos's body. Her laughter shifted into a maniacal cackle possessed by unrest and grief.

"This will shut you up, whore," Krazh shouted. His sword shimmered in the starlight, and the moon reflected a flash of light. The sun had finally sunk, and the entire world went black.

Rumbling thunder crashed in a cloudless sky. A vacuous wind blew through the dusty streets. The stars in the night were gone, and the moon had dilated like a cyclops peering down on decay. A glowing beam of blacklight shot into Krazh, and his body surged with brilliant electric colors. He convulsed and oozed with black liquid from all of his orifices. His arms and legs, then his chest, rapidly swelled into blistering boils and, finally, burst from the inside. Globs of brain matter, and organs slopped on the remaining soldiers behind him. As his skeleton stood momentarily before crumbling to dust, whisked away with the wind, his sword chimed dropping to the ground.

A hazy candescent tint masked my vision. The bodies of the Mgozk started to rise from their deathbeds, dismembered and grotesque. The head of Zelmoda lifted off the ground and hovered through the streets. Her decapitated head circled by black fire and glowed with those electric colors. "Skul," the head of Zelmoda whispered. "Skul."

The reanimated corpses of the Mgozk repeated, "skul!"

Thousands of chattering voices began to chant the prayer that Elosinda had spoken before Krazh's untimely death. Louder and louder, I heard those names being whispered in the wind.

Tulzscha. Uvhash. Ycnagnnissz...

I looked up and saw a crack in the sky before the giant black monolith. A fissure torn open by something I cannot put a name to. Energy pulsed through the monolith and a melodic buzzing sound erupted from the opening like a choir of insects. The soldiers threw their hands against their ears, but it could not stop the process. The cycle the Mgo was celebrating. The Black Sails had begun. The heads of the soldiers melted down into a coagulated slime and ran down the bloody stumps on their necks. Headless bodies dropped like piles of g'lac shit. It was the finale in a symphony as the g'lacs trampled the corpses. I wouldn't call myself lucky, but I was alive.

They chanted.

In a thousand voices.

Coming toward me.

Tulzscha. Uvhash. Ycnagnnissz...

I did the only thing I could think of...

I pointed my camera before me, and hit the shutter.

I'M NOT certain how I arrived on the steps of The Kastle. Suspended in a perpetual hangover, I waited for the State-boys to bring me inside. Figured The Man would want to see some kind of report.

An investigation of the campaign did not provide sufficient data for them or myself. The Man sent out a team of scientists to the Outlands, but they cannot explain what happened to the Mgozk or their city.

There was nothing left. The Man was most concerned with the black monolith that had seemed to have never existed.

Developing the photographs did not give much more insight either. I'm not sure what I had photographed.

Proof?

The Kastle seized the photographs once they were delivered, but they didn't agree with the narrative it suggested and they did not want that kind of information escaping to the disillusioned public. It was told that the campaign was a complete success. The photographs were destroyed and replaced by the propaganda of Mgozk cannibalism and bestiality.

I still made the front page.

Reporter Survives Cannibal-Rape Massacre...

The Man gave me an honorable discharge for my service and they made me out like some sort of hero. I was not used to the luxury and it helped suffocate the swelling grief of the atrocities I had been a part of.

They provided me with a new apartment on one of their higher floors in The Kastle. The balcony overlooked the crowded skyline that tangled and twisted with steel obelisks. It was nice for a while until one long night of drinking plenty of ale. I had finished twelve horns sitting on the balcony. I grabbed my last one and everytime I took a swig, a faint whisper came from behind me, louder with each drink.

"Skul," the voice said. I couldn't ignore it anymore.

"Who's there?" I finally snapped around, spilling the last drops of my ale. And there they were.

Elosinda faint apparition was holding her boy.

Elos frowned at me. He clicked his tongue and motioned his hands up to his face like he was taking a photograph.

I shook my head and rubbed my eyes. Elos dropped from his mother's side and walked toward me. His body, stained with crusty blood, floated toward me with something in his hand.

"Skul," Elos said.

He handed me a photograph in his hand. I only caught a glimpse of it and what I saw sent me running toward the balcony in hopes of leaping over the railing. I screamed. My skeleton ejected from my throat. I made it to the balcony, but a doctor busted through my door with a staff of nurses. They must have heard my screams. The entire top floor had to hear me. They stormed me, secured me down and a needle penetrated my neck.

I fell to the floor.

The next day I woke up in a daze and a nurse informed me that I should forget about Mgo. I was going through severe grieving. My mind wasn't right. They gave me some pills. Blue and yellow ones.

"Take Xantrol in the morning and Orzak at night." She nodded and glanced around her shoulder to see if any of her superiors were around. "You know, I take both at night. It won't hurt you. It will make you feel better than you've ever felt in your life."

She was right.

Never felt better.

ACKNOWLEDGMENTS

Thanks to Brittany, Taj, and Soren. My family, my only reason for being alive. Thanks to Nat and Cousin Taylor, you all have inspired much of the content in these stories. Thanks Nathan for reading the early drafts of these stories., too.

Thanks to the Void Collective (Evan Dean Shelton, Matthew Mitchell, Justin Lutz, Sam Richard, and Michael Tichy), I appreciate you all for having faith in these stories. Thanks to Courtney Pierce for the constant encouragement and always helping out when I need to figure out how to computer things.

Thanks to Coy Hall, Damien Casey, John Wayne Comunale, and Scott Bryan Wilson for checking out this collection and the nice words.

Other than that, there's nothing else to say.

I can offer empty thank yous left and right to more people I dont know and to make them feel special but that just seems so ingenuine.

These stories mean nothing in the end.

Time itself may not be linear in the three-lobed eye of the universe but for our microcosmic existence it is.

It has a definite end.

And if were lucky the universe does, too.

ABOUT THE AUTHOR

Edwin Callihan is a liar. Edwin Callihan wrote this book.

THE IMPERIAL DYNASTY OF TRUE WEIRD &HORROR

HISTORIES OF MGO BY EDWIN CALLIHAN $14.99

A DIVER, A DEMON BY CHRISTA PAGLIEI $19.99

VOIDHAUS BY THE VOID COLLECTIVE $10.99

CHURCHBURNER BY EVAN DEAN SHELTON $13.99

GEMINI RISING BY JUSTIN LUTZ $9.99

WOUND OF THE WEST BY MICHAEL TICHY $6.66

BEHIND EVERY TREE BENEATH EVERY ROCK
BY MICHAEL TICHY $11.99

BASS TAPE MASSACRE, VOL. 1: LOW FREQUENCY
BY BREONNA HYPE $9.99

MARU KIRU, DESTROY THE MOON, VOL 1
BY BRENDAN ALBETSKI $9.99

LOCKDOWN LAUREATE BY O.F. CIERI $14.99

INTRO TO THE CRYPT OF RAYS BY VARIOUS $14.99

THE VOID BECKONS TO US ALL. NO ONE ESCAPES THE SIREN'S CALL. HEED NOW AND REAP YOUR ETERNAL REWARD.
IT IS AS EASY AS FILLING OUT AND MAILING IN THE FORM BELOW TO CASTAIGNEPUBLISHING@GMAIL.COM.

Name____

Address____

City___________________________________Zip____________

E-mail____